ISBN 978-1-331-80086-6
PIBN 10236465

This book is a reproduction of an important historical work. Forgotten Books uses state-of-the-art technology to digitally reconstruct the work, preserving the original format whilst repairing imperfections present in the aged copy. In rare cases, an imperfection in the original, such as a blemish or missing page, may be replicated in our edition. We do, however, repair the vast majority of imperfections successfully; any imperfections that remain are intentionally left to preserve the state of such historical works.

1 MONTH OF
FREE
READING

at
www.ForgottenBooks.com

By purchasing this book you are eligible for one month membership to ForgottenBooks.com, giving you unlimited access to our entire collection of over 700,000 titles via our web site and mobile apps.

To claim your free month visit:
www.forgottenbooks.com/free236465

English
Français
Deutsche
Italiano
Español
Português

www.forgottenbooks.com

Mythology Photography **Fiction**
Fishing Christianity **Art** Cooking
Essays Buddhism Freemasonry
Medicine **Biology** Music **Ancient
Egypt** Evolution Carpentry Physics
Dance Geology **Mathematics** Fitness
Shakespeare **Folklore** Yoga Marketing
Confidence Immortality Biographies
Poetry **Psychology** Witchcraft
Electronics Chemistry History **Law**
Accounting **Philosophy** Anthropology
Alchemy Drama Quantum Mechanics
Atheism Sexual Health **Ancient History**
Entrepreneurship Languages Sport
Paleontology Needlework Islam
Metaphysics Investment Archaeology
Parenting Statistics Criminology
Motivational

TALES FROM THE RUSSIAN.

TALES FROM THE RUSSIAN

OF

MME. KABALENSKY.

TRANSLATED BY G. JENNER.

LONDON:

BLACKIE & SON, 49 & 50 OLD BAILEY, E.C.
GLASGOW, EDINBURGH, AND DUBLIN.

CONTENTS.

SILVER DEW.

AM still a very little girl, and really a very happy one. Every one loves me; and as for my dear mama, how tenderly she caresses me, and how pleasant it is for me to sleep on her knees! But I had better begin to tell you what lately happened to me.

One evening mama was sitting in the nursery sewing, whilst I was busy drawing, seated on my little chair beside her. That was a very pleasant evening for me, for mama told me a great many pretty stories. We sat long together, and when it grew late I began to feel very sleepy. Then mama put down her work, took me on her knees, and sang my pet song. I enjoyed it very much, my room is so neat and pleasant, mama is so kind and her voice so gentle. I felt so cosy lying in mama's arms listening to her dear singing, and gazing at the large silver image that stands in the corner, lighted up by the brightly burning lamp in its blue crystal vase. I went on opening and shutting my eyes, and each time the blue vase seemed brighter and brighter, and the rays from the little lamp grew longer and longer until they seemed to reach mama's head. Meanwhile she sang:—

Sleep, my dearest, quick to rest;
Sleep, my babe, till break of day;
Joy to-morrow fill thy breast;
Rise, at morn, with fancies gay.

Sleep, my love, to thee will bring
Guardian angels, wonders rare;
To my sleeping dove will sing
Of the heavens so bright and fair.

How they watch the stars at play,
And the golden moon they view
Bathe, when night succeeds to day,
In a flood of silver dew.

The rays from the blue vase were now so long that they reached to the other end of the room, and surrounded mama's head with a bright glory, and ever ringing in my ears I heard, "in a flood of silver dew."

Then I thought to myself how lovely must silver dew be, and I longed to be the moon that I might bathe in it. Suddenly I became aware that the rays from the lamp no longer shook, but had taken the form of a flight of silver steps. I stretched out my hand and felt that they were quite firm, and that they reached upwards higher than I could see. I resolved to try if they would bear me. I did so, and then began to climb them in perfect safety.

The higher I climbed the brighter and bluer shone the light, and I thought to myself, "I am going to the moon to bathe in silver dew. How delightful it will be, and how I shall like to learn the moon's way of living!"

I climbed the silver steps for a long time before they came to an end. I stopped on the last landing and looked about me. Before me stretched an immense garden full of the strangest trees. I hadn't the least idea where to go, nor what to see. Before me lay a number of paths, and those paths were sprinkled—guess with what? With silver dew. How I longed to bathe my face in it, but I couldn't manage it; it was spread out all over the path, and I didn't like to stop long enough to collect it. So I resolved to run on further to see the beautiful garden and find more silver dew. I chose the path straight before me and ran on. Now this path was so narrow that my frock touched the flowers which grew on each side of it. To my wonder they began to nod and to give forth the sweetest songs and music. All the flowers sang, and so beauti- fully! Never before had I heard such silvery voices. They sang of the games of the stars, and of the bathing of the moon. I was so delighted with their songs that I went on running for a long time without feeling tired. At last I stopped to look at the lovely singing flowers; I knelt down, and taking hold of one of them very gently I looked into her little cup. Then only I found out that there were a great many silver bells with tiny golden clappers in each flower, and these, at the slightest touch, began ringing and singing.

I longed to gather one of them, but I felt it would be a pity to destroy its song, so I sat down upon the path and passed my hand lightly over the flowers. They began singing again, and then I also saw that as long as I kept them moving drops of silver dew kept constantly flowing from them. I then understood why the whole path was sprinkled with it.

Still I was very anxious to know the moon, or at least to watch the stars at play; so I went straight on, the singing sounding louder and clearer at each step. At last, at the end of a path I saw a strange-looking summer-house. It was nothing but the shell of an enormous blue egg. I longed to enter it, and after some search I found that the entrance was overgrown by a bush covered with white blossoms. I squeezed my way through the branches until I reached the doorway. Looking in I saw a beautiful girl lying on a bed of rose leaves, sleeping most sweetly; a large white swan sat near her, fanning her with his wings, for it was really very hot. How pretty she looked! But I could not see what her clothes were made of; they were as transparent as clouds, and all sprinkled with silver dew. She had a pair of folded snow-white wings, and wore on her head a complete crown of stars.

When I entered the pavilion the sleeper unfolded her wings and opened her eyes, much surprised at seeing me there. She asked me how I had got there, and I told her everything that had happened to me. She asked me very kindly what I wished to do next.

"I wish to make the acquaintance of the moon, and to see the stars at play," answered I, "if you will kindly allow me."

"Not only will I allow you, but I will myself show you everything. I am a star princess, and the moon is my father. Come with me. It is already twilight; you know that we none of us can go out in the daylight. When the twilight comes the evening breeze plays over the flowers, and they awaken us with their ringing and singing, and then we go out to play and enjoy ourselves in the garden. Our father the moon comes out from his palace, and we pass the time with him most gaily."

"How strange!" cried I. "With us it is just the contrary; we move about all day and we sleep at night."

"Yes, I know that," answered the princess; "we know everything that takes place on the earth; and at night my father looks down upon your homes, to see if everything is in order and if any one is in need of light. He knows that at night it is dark on the earth, and does his best to light up mankind."

"I know, I know it," said I. "I have often seen your father and all of you in the sky at night, but so far off that I could not examine you nicely."

As we were speaking, we went out into the garden again, and there I saw a number of beautiful girls; they were all nearly as lovely as my dear princess, and they all wore stars on their heads, some of them only one, and others a complete crown. Their dresses were all strewn with silver dew.

Some of them flew through the air in groups, whilst others ran along the paths so lightly that they didn't stir the flowers enough to make them sing.

We came out into a meadow, and there, on the

borders of a large blue lake, stood an immense crystal palace decorated with garlands of white flowers. The least breath of wind set the silver bells of the flowers ringing, and from their cups whole cascades of silver dew flowed into the lake. I could not take my eyes off the palace, when all of a sudden I heard a sound like the distant rumbling of thunder. The princesses began to move up and down, and I saw that each of them held in her hand a large white flower, in the midst of which burnt a brilliant flame. The stars on their heads also began to throw out rays in all directions, the lake and the palace shone with a bright light, and from the gate of the latter a golden boat, in which was seated an old man with curly white locks, floated into the lake. The boat was drawn by a white swan linked to it by a silver chain. When it reached the middle of a lake all the princesses with their bright torches flew towards it, and I remained alone on the bank.

I longed to fly with them, but, alas! I had no wings. Suddenly a swan alighted close to me and stretched out his wings. I understood at once that he would take me on his back. I took my place between his wings, embracing his downy neck, and we flew out to the middle of the lake. I was longing to see the moon bathe. Meanwhile the star princesses went on with their games. They formed a large group, and their dresses spread round them in a cloud as they moved from side to side, whilst bright sparks of fire seemed to fall from their torches upon the water.

The moon floated calmly upon the water, directing the white swan. I flew after him, watching for the moment when he would bathe. At length a light mist spread over the sky, the lake assumed a rosy hue, and I saw that the golden boat was floating back towards the palace.

I had already made up my mind that I should see nothing more, that it was not true that the moon would bathe, when what I so much wished for took place.

The boat stopped at the very gates of the crystal palace; the moon laid down the reins he was holding, and the swan ceased moving. All the princesses formed a large circle round the lake, a fresh breeze sprang up, the flowers burst into song, the little bells began to ring, everything was in motion; from every garland, from the walls of the palace, and from the cups of the flowers flowed a prodigious quantity of silver dew. The boat was half-filled with it; the moon lay down and began to bathe; the princesses all floated over him, and with their quivering wings sprinkled the cold silver dew upon him. It was scattered about in such quantities that I upon my white bird was wet through and through with it, until I felt such pleasure and such delightful coolness as it is impossible for me to describe.

And then—I woke suddenly. I opened my eyes and could understand nothing. I was lying on my little bed in my own room. I at once looked at the lamp to see if the silver steps were still there. There was no longer any trace of them. But through the open window I could hear the morning song of the birds; the lime-tree which overshadowed the house was wet with rain-drops, and whenever a gust of wind entered the room the cold damp blossoms came with it. They strewed the window-sill, the floor, and even my bed. The day was hot, and the room full of the perfume of the flowers.

What is it all, then? Have I really not bathed in silver dew? But my face is still wet, my hair is full of lime blossoms. Ah! I know all about it now. Mama has been here, and has opened the window gently that the birds might awaken me. I must have been asleep.

Well, it makes no difference. I can tell now how delightful it must be to bathe in "silver dew."

THE CRIMSON TOADSTOOL.

A LADY-BIRD was running hurriedly towards a neighbouring hillock; she was in great alarm, and could hardly get over the different obstacles she met with on her road. Her red gown, marked with little black spots, was all in disorder; it was half open, and one transparent wing hung out. It was clearly to be seen from her attire that something had alarmed her, and that she had forgotten to fold the delicate tissue of her wings. Out of breath, stumbling and tripping at each step, she climbed up the hill, and, stopping beneath the green moss, hardly waited to regain her breath before she hailed her neighbour.

"Where are you, little neighbour?" she screamed; "come out quick!"

At her voice appeared from beneath the green moss a neatly-dressed little lady, with black specks on her yellow gown. The neighbour was also a lady-bird.

B

"What has happened?" said she, pushing out her head from between two tufts of moss which looked like tiny firs.

"A misfortune, dear friend," cried the red one. "Without taking breath I ran to you, without even dressing myself properly."

"But what's the matter? tell me, quick."

"A fearful occurrence, neighbour; I can hardly relate it. We were all sitting peaceably on our hillock, under the fir-tree over there, each of us at her own work, when suddenly—oh! 'twas fearful, I can't bear to remember it—our native hillock began to move as if it were swelling, and the ground beneath our feet cracked with such a noise! A whole mass of moss was torn up! so that we could no longer keep our footing. Oh! it was terrible; I have not recovered yet."

"What an event!" said the astonished yellow one; "but you must have seen something if you only looked."

"How could we look?" retorted the red one. "We all ran away in a fright as quick as we could. And now what is to be done? there are nests and eggs everywhere, you know; where can we go at this time of year?"

"There is no use in worrying one s self before the time," answered the wise yellow one; "you must wait, and then it will be as God decides. At all events, let us go and see." And they both set off.

From afar off they became aware of a fearful disturbance. The people were flying from the hillock, each carrying away what he could lay hands on; this one a grain, that one an egg, whilst a third clutched a leaf larger than himself; all ran without looking back, pushing one another. The confusion was terrible, and it was evident that the nation had run wild with fear

One of the younger ones who had climbed a shrub and could not hold on at the top, rolled head-over-heels downwards. They were all so dismayed that the winged inhabitants forgot to avail themselves of the privilege nature had granted to them, and instead of unfolding their wings and taking flight, were pushing about amidst the runners, adding to the general confusion.

"Good gracious! how am I to manage with my little children?" screamed the red lady-bird; and, filled with despair, she rolled upon the ground with her legs uppermost. The yellow one was already much disturbed, and glanced stealthily in the direction of her own hillock, but all was quiet there.

"But, my dear friend," expostulated she in an uneasy tone, "all this grief will not help; to kill

yourself will only make things worse. This is a
punishment for our sins. Alas! we have sinned."

"But what is to be done?" groaned the red
one. "Where can I rest my head now? It's destruction and nothing else."

"Stand up, get upon your feet!" continued her
comforter, "God is over everything. Now come
along with me, we have seen together what has
happened;" and she dragged off her sorrow-stricken
companion.

Much did the neighbours converse, and much
the people wept. The destruction was general, the
silence of death reigned over the desolated spot,
interrupted only from time to time by the cracking of the ground; the moss was thrown back
more and more, whole tufts of it, torn up from
the soil, rolled down the hillock; not one inhabi-
tant was left. In the evening, when all the
fugitives had found room in the neighbouring
hillocks, the youth assembled and began to discuss
the terrible event, and as the first panic had
subsided some young beetles proposed to their
comrades to approach the dangerous spot and
observe the neighbourhood. The old beetles
tried to dissuade them, and the lady-birds would
not hear of any one even showing his nose in
that direction. But a daring green beetle held
his own, and with a band of his bolder compan-

ions resolved to make his way to the spot. It was agreed that a winged ant should be sent on in front to reconnoitre, not on foot, but flying, and keeping at a certain height, so that in the event of danger he could return in the same manner.

Our ant equipped himself and set out. The whole youth of the community awaited his return at the edge of the hillock where the tiny fir-trees ended, and a smooth velvet sward of moss began.

The messenger soon returned and reported that all was quiet there, but that he had seen from afar something awful, the earth was red-dening like fire, but there was no one.

The daring ones looked at one another, and for some time remained irresolute, but they soon grew ashamed of their cowardice and firmly resolved that before sunset the whole company should have reached the dreadful spot.

No sooner said than done. The assembly in a troop started in that direction.

When they arrived near the hillock they halted and stood listening; "Gently!" the green beetle, as the bravest, climbed up and cried out; "let those who are not cowards follow me." The blood flew to the youths' heads, and with one accord they rushed up the hillock.

Hardly had they reached the top than a rumbling sound was heard, the earth opened. "Out of the way!" screamed an awful voice; and from the ground appeared a tall, stout, and lobster-red toadstool, a tattered white cloak alone covered his loins, he wore his hat viciously cocked, and with arms akimbo, and swelling haughtily, he surveyed the neighbourhood.

At this sight the youth tumbled head-over-heels down the hillock, and without another glance scattered in all directions with intense fear and trembling.

"Be off from this hillock!" shrieked the toad-stool fiercely, swelling and reddening more and more. Our heroes already felt their legs sinking under them. The fungus saw this, but chose to brag and overwhelm them with terror.

The young beetles returned home intoxicated with alarm, and fell senseless on the moss, with their legs in the air.

"Terrible, terrible!" lamented the lady-birds, "when will these horrors cease? The end of the world must be near! Alas for our poor little heads!"

Long they mourned over their terror-stricken youth, and the popular agitation only began to subside when the moon had already risen high in the heavens and the cool dew had refreshed the heated brains of the people. At last all was quiet.

The night was calm and the stars shone brightly, the clear light of the moon cast a silvery radiance on the scattered flowers and the white trunks of the curly birches, whose long and slender branches waved in the night air and shed sleep and calm upon the living; noiselessly floated the silver moon in the clear blue sky; noiselessly twinkled the brilliant stars in the transparent heavens; noiselessly the flowers gave forth their perfumes, filling the air with their fragrance.

A poor withered plant nodded its languid head, sleeping in the general silence. It waited its hour calmly and resignedly.

From time to time the earth round the red toadstool rumbled; but there he stood, with arms akimbo, full of gravity, casting a contemptuous glance at the plant which was bending down to the earth. But sleep at last overcame him; he fell asleep without changing his position, and without observing how the calm starry night pensively dropped tears on his insolent loutish head.

The sky was beginning to darken, the moon sank beneath the edge of the earth; the stars paled, and in the east appeared a bright pink band of light. The wind blew lightly over the sleeping kingdom of flowers and insects; the flowers awoke and turned their heads tenderly towards the pink band of light. The whole vicinity was lighted up by rosy flames, a cloud with gilded edges floated through the sky, and the mist rising from the earth gave chase to it.

Everything in the wood awoke, the birds sang, the insects began to move, a little squirrel with a bushy tail climbed up a birch-tree, from which he leaped to a fir, and scrambling to the top of it cocked up his ears. The hares with bated breath bounded across the road, over the meadow, to the neighbouring rill. The redwing whistled here and there in the thicket. The gnats, beetles, and lady-birds were all astir.

The little plant stretched out its weary head and looked at the toadstool. There he stood redder than ever; his hat was covered with little white knobs, he was more puffed out than before, and had climbed still further out of the earth. His size and proportions were alarming even to the sparrows, and the lady-birds when they came out in the morning to bathe in the dew were mute with terror. The crimson monster was already visible from their hillocks.

"What a visitation!" said they to one another in a cautious whisper. "How can it have grown up? Such a sight was never seen;" and they all rushed in alarm into the middle of the hillock.

In the morning the young beetles were much ashamed of the cowardice they had displayed the evening before, and knew not how to face the scornful looks of their neighbours. After much deliberation they agreed to march up to the fungus, be it understood without approaching too near.

On hearing of the preparations the lady-bird resolved to drag herself after them. She had left all her household belongings on the hillock, and she wished to see, at least from afar, if nothing could be saved. And so, without giving notice to any one, she slipped off between the tufts of moss and hid herself not far from the terrible hillock.

But from the height at which the crimson monster stood everything was visible. He observed at once the bands of youths and the lady-bird.

"Do not advance," he growled, "or I will poison you all."

The beetles halted, but did not retreat. The green one stood out from the crowd. "You insolent wretch, don't you know who I am? I'm the *crimson fly-killing agaric*. And who is that? What baggage is hidden there in the red gown? Get out, you good-for-nothing!"

The beetles were dreadfully afraid, though they did not show it, but gazed from afar at the enraged monster. The lady-bird climbed up a hillock and hid under a tiny fir-tree. But the plant listened to everything attentively and only shook her head in thought; it was evident that her reflections were very deep.

The beetles retired, making believe that they were taking a stroll and saw nothing to fear.

The rain began to fall, all the living inhabitants sought shelter where they could. The toadstool stood up proudly, his arms akimbo, and laughing with wide-opened mouth at the alarm of the common people. The rain fell in torrents on his elastic head and ran down his legs in complete cascades, but his hat only grew the redder. And now the sun set, but the rain did not cease. The whole country seemed covered with a winding-sheet, everything was wonderfully still, only near the mushroom was heard the noise of water, as if from a water-spout. Thus the whole night passed.

In the morning the sky cleared up, and every one came out of his hiding-place.

The youths assembled on the top of their hillocks to observe the crimson toadstool from a height.

"Help me!" was suddenly heard in his rough voice; "brethren, help; gnats, beetles, and lady-birds, I am falling!"

The people were scattered all over the hillocks, filled with terror. They all looked in the direction whence the voice came.

"I am falling, I am falling completely," cried the despairing fungus. And, indeed, it was evident that he was bending over to one side; his hat had fallen off upon his shoulders, his face was contracted and blue.

Regardless of danger, a party of young beetles rushed towards him; but before they could scramble up the hillock he sank heavily in the mud.

"I am done for," groaned he in a deep bass voice; "I am altogether done for."

And in truth that very day there was an end of the valiant warrior. In the evening you could no longer tell where his face had been, and where his hat; nothing was left of him but a little heap of slimy mud. But the little plant waved its head, and thought mighty thoughts.

"How much evil!" thought she; "he defiles the earth, poisons the air, and fills the inhabitants with terror and grief. Oh! if it were but given me to root out evil and establish good!"

A last bitter tear dropped from her closing eyes; with a feeble effort she drew from her heart her best seed, and threw it on the slimy heap, which was all that remained of Fly-killer.

The summer passed, and the winter passed too. The inhabitants of the hillocks awoke from their winter rest, and gazed joyfully at God's world. The beetles and lady-birds assembled to rejoice on the old hillock; but they resolved to begin by examining the spot where the dreaded toadstool had been. They all collected round their birthplace; but what was the sight that met their eyes?

In the place of the terrible crimson fungus, a lily of the valley. She stood erect, stretching out her broad, dark leaves, and only waving one little branch covered with hanging white blossoms. She looked at them all caressingly and joyfully.

"Come to me, all of you," said she, stretching out her broad arms; "I am placed here for you; and as long as I live my leaves will give you coolness and shade, and my flowers juice and honey. I will fill the air with fragrance. I will give you shelter under the shade of my leaves. I will give you my heart and my life, if they be needed. Oh, come, come under my shade!"

The insects all greeted her joyfully, and accepted her caressing proposals.

And that hillock, they say, is the very happiest and most favoured spot in the whole wood.

THE NIGHTINGALE'S NOTES.

IN a thick wood, on the border of a mere overgrown with reeds and yellow lilies, there stood a huge old tree. The whole of its trunk was covered with moss, and on its branches were a number of birds' nests not long since abandoned by their inhabitants. The grass beneath the tree was strewn with the broken shells of the eggs of various birds. The tree was so old that its trunk contained a deep hollow. In this cavity lay a bundle of carefully-arranged maple leaves bound together by long marsh-grass. On these leaves was written the story of a nightingale. Would not some one like to read it? Here it is.

I remember well my early youth as far back as the time when I had attained the age of ten days. Yes, I can clearly recall one morning when I awoke sitting in the nest, with my little legs tucked under me, trembling with cold. The morning was fresh, the wind was blowing, and I felt fearfully chilly in my light clothing of soft gray down.

When fully aroused, I began chirping most plaintively from cold. I must have been very silly then, not to guess that I ought to squeeze myself under my mother's wings. But as soon as I began complaining, mama herself took me carefully by the neck and placed me under her warm, fluffy wings. I got warm at once, and fell asleep again.

When I awoke the sun was already high in the heavens, and mama was sitting on the edge of the nest singing sweetly. I looked at her, and felt surprised that she could produce such wonderful sounds. I longed to try and sing myself, but I only succeeded in screaming lustily and disturbing mama. She turned to me at once and said:

"Sit still, little birdie, and don't scream so loud; you are growing big now, and should look after the younger children."

She arranged my down with her beak, replaced the hanging straw in the nest, smoothed her own wing, and plucking out a few feathers placed them in the nest. Then I saw that mama was tending my sisters, whom I had not remarked at all. They must, indeed, have come out of the eggs much later than I; but I was so young myself that I could not, as yet, help mama to look after them. But, seeing what trouble she took, I felt it a shame to do nothing but scream and disturb her, and with a sudden hop I found myself close to my little sisters. I at once wished to pluck out some little feathers and put them under them; but no sooner did I begin to pull at my down than I felt such pain that I began screaming louder than before, and felt greatly terrified. Mama flew at once to me to look at the sore place. I was so ashamed! How am I to keep from screaming and disturbing poor mama? thought I; and I firmly resolved to sit still.

Having seated us in the nest, mama said to me:

"Now, little nightingale, I must fly away to get food for you. You must try and be good, and keep the little ones warm; they are still so silly that they may climb out of the nest if you don't keep them from the edge."

"Very well," said I, "I will try and be good; fly away comfortably and don't be anxious about the children."

Mama flew once more round the nest to give a good look at us, burst into a musical song and soared upwards, high above the trees. She was soon lost from my sight in the blue sky above.

Then, for the first time, I resolved to risk myself on the edge of the nest and look about me. I saw, for the first time, that the thick mass of green that surrounded us was pierced by a small window, from which a most beautiful view was to be had.

Before me stretched a large mere. It was perfectly smooth, and reflected the trees which surrounded it. On its banks grew thick grasses and tall green reeds, and on the water itself floated large, glossy green leaves with bright yellow flowers. Farther out bloomed a quantity of white water-lilies. I looked down into one of them, and observed that it was full of water. The sun played upon that water until it shone so that my eyes were hurt, and I nearly began to cry again; but I remembered mama's words and restrained myself.

I sat long in the nest looking at my sisters, but mama did not come. At last I grew anxious, and began to think that she had really entirely forgotten us.

Meanwhile the sun became hidden by clouds, and the trees began to move; a cold wind blew, and the water of the mere was set in motion. I drew closer to my sisters, and began trembling from alarm and cold. The wind grew stronger, our nest was violently rocked, and at last shook us so much that I began crying out from fear. My sisters got up and did the same. I knew not where to fly for refuge, and anxiously awaited mama's arrival. We all kept up a terrible scream- ing, when suddenly I heard the water splash close to us and saw a huge green frog. How spiteful she seemed! Opening her eyes wide, she looked at us, and instead of feeling pity for us poor little ones she set up a loud croaking. We became silent from fright; but she went on croaking: "Horrid little screechers! horrid little scree-ee-chers!"

Fortunately at this moment I heard my mother's chirp, and saw her close to the nest. She was so tired that she could hardly move her wings; but, not thinking of herself, she sat down in the nest, stretched out her wings, and gathering us all under them she began to distribute to us small flies and worms, of which she had collected a sufficient stock for our breakfast. After feed- ing us she arranged the nest with her beak, and I looked to see if the spiteful frog were still there.

He was looking at us with his goggle eyes. At that moment there came a flash of lightning, and a loud peal of thunder was heard. The frog at once hopped down the bank and disappeared in the water.

I told mama all that had happened to us. She was very indignant at the frog's conduct, but added that there was nothing to fear from him. "He is always scolding and loves to croak, but he can't hurt you in the least," said mama; and then told me to shelter myself beneath her wings.

Hardly was I comfortably settled than the tree began to creak again, and heavy drops of rain fell pattering on the leaves. "'Tis well," thought I, "that our nest is concealed in such a thicket, or the rain would undoubtedly have drenched us." Even as it was, from time to time I was sprinkled with tiny rain-drops strained through the overhanging leaves. The noise was fearful. The mere became of a dark-blue colour and was covered with huge bubbles, the frogs were silenced, and the yellow and white flowers were forced beneath the surface by the weight of the torrents of rain.

For a long time nothing was heard but the rushing of the water and the rustling of the leaves. All the inhabitants of the wood were silenced. From time to time the lightning flashed, and the deep roar of the thunder filled the wood. But we were so warm and comfortable under mama's wings that we all fell asleep.

Mama's loud singing awoke us, and on arousing myself I nearly fainted with joy. How beautiful

everything had become! The storm had ceased,
the sky was of a vivid blue, the air was calm,
and the sun shone brightly, reflected by the rain-
drops attached to every blade of grass, and to
the leaves of every tree. I thought each leaf
was a large shining star. The smell of the damp
earth, and of the yellow flowers which grew
near us, arose on every side. The mere was
covered with glossy, silvery froth, the large
white lilies floated calmly on the surface of the
water. Songs resounded on every side, but I
could not understand who sang so beautifully.
Mama was perched on the highest branch of the
hazel-tree where we lived, drying her feathers
with a quivering motion, which shook off the
drops of rain from them. "Mama," said I, "who
is it that sings so loudly? I hear a voice from
every bush, but can see no one."

"Those are our neighbours," answered mama.
"We don't live here alone. This is a very agreeable
place of residence. A number of birds have lived
here for years like myself, and others fly here
from time to time, but we are all acquainted, and
I know the history of each of my neighbours as
well as that of the bushes in which they live.
Your birthplace is a charming spot, little nightingale; you will certainly be as fond of the
mere and its banks as I am. I may truly say

that I prefer this place to any in which I have been."

"I suppose there is nothing elsewhere so pretty as this mere, mama," said I.

"On the contrary," answered she, "there are many prettier places, and in some of the more distant ones life is easier, because the weather is always hot. But I like this mere the best, for it was here I first broke my way out of the shell, and saw for the first time God's glorious world; here I first began to understand the meaning of everything, and grew attached to my good neighbours. Lastly, little nightingale, it was here I first met your father. I loved him fondly; and since that time this mere has been dearer to me than all the world besides. Here I first had children, and found food for them, after settling in these hazel-bushes, where I could build a nest protected from the weather. In one word, here I first came to the understanding of everything, and learned to love God's universe. My dearly beloved mere, I shall never forget thee, my beautiful birthplace, where all things are dear to me, the hazel-bushes and ranunculuses, the old hollow tree, and my neighbours, all things, all things!"

I listened to mama with the deepest attention. She was so happy that whilst I was gazing at her she burst, all at once, into the most melodious song. Seated on a branch she produced from her throat the most harmonious sounds; raising her beak towards the sky and shaking her head, she sang on without interruption a song of her happiness; meanwhile from a large maple leaf ran a slender, glistening stream of rain, which splashed upon the branch where mama was sitting, but she observed nothing.

I sat and thought of the countries where it is always hot, wishing much to go and visit them. "Mama," asked I, "shall we ever see a place where it will always be warm?"

Mama was silent at once and hung down her head. After a little while she said: "Don't speak to me, birdie, of such sad things. I try not to think of them before the time, and meanwhile let us be happy in our dear home. Let us try and forget that the sad time for abandoning it must come only too soon."

I became silent at once, not to annoy her, but my heart beat with excitement, for I longed ardently to see hot countries. It is true that as yet I had hardly seen my own at all, and only knew our single bush and the yellow ranunculuses that grew close to it. Still it seemed to me that wonders were only to be found far away in hot countries.

Meanwhile day succeeded day and we all lived

in our nest.   I grew rapidly enough, and I began
to observe that my down was no longer always
ruffled, but was taking to lie smooth, and that
numbers of gray feathers were making their
appearance.

"I must be very pretty," thought I.   I wanted
to see if I was like mama.   I soon guessed how
to manage it.   Mama already allowed me to fly
out of the nest, and I found out myself how to
do it.

When I was still a little thing she used to take
me on her back, fly out of the nest, and, circling
a little in the air, suddenly alight upon the
ground.   After this I soon learned to use my
wings, and little by little taught myself to fly.

And so I flew cautiously to the very edge of the
mere, perched on the top of a large fern which
overhung the water, and, bending my head, began
to look down into its depths.   But how ridicu-
lous!   I saw that I was not at all like mama.
Many of my feathers stuck out at the sides, and
my head seemed enormous.   On becoming aware
of my deformity I felt deeply pained, and sank
down in complete silence.   Suddenly I heard a
voice, and, turning round, I saw looking at me
with caressing eyes, a lovely bird, who asked me
why I wore such a sad air.   "I have been here
a long time looking for food," continued she.

"and I ought already to be at home; but your sorrow pains me, dear little nightingale, you are so young, and I can't bear to see children unhappy, my own or those of others; I love them all."

"I don't know your name," said I.

"I am called Goldfinch," answered my new acquaintance, "and I wish you, darling, to be frank with me."

"How kind you are, dear Goldfinch! don't pay attention to my sadness; I'm silly, that's all. I fancied myself like mama, and when I looked into the water I saw that I was not at all like her, and I felt disappointed." With these words I hung down my head and pecked a little at my ruffled feathers.

"Poor little thing!" said the Goldfinch kindly. "Don't let that trouble you. In the first place, you are not grown up as yet, so you can't be quite like your mother, whom I know well. Besides which, appearances are nothing. Be as kind and good as other nightingales are, and every one will certainly love you. In time you also will charm us all with your beautiful voice."

"Shall I ever be able to sing like my father?" asked I. "He sings at night in such a manner that all the birds listen to him without stirring from their places for fear of interrupting him."

"No, my darling," answered the Goldfinch,

"you will whistle like your mother, for wives can't sing like their husbands, brothers, and fathers; nor is it necessary for them to do so, they have nobler work than singing. When you are grown up and have your own nest you will have to look after the children. Just imagine what it must be to hatch a whole brood, and how much trouble is required to bring up, as your mother does, an entire family. You must understand, too, how difficult it must be to build the nest, to lay all the eggs, to hatch you all, and above all to preserve you from hunger and cold, from the wind and the rain, and from dangerous neighbours. Oh, no, you can't understand how much there is to be done, or how happy your mother, will be when she sees you all full-grown and pretty nightingales. She is a most careful mother and a very good bird. I love and respect her exceedingly. Yes, every one respects her, even the cuckoo, who is too lazy to bring up her own children, and places her eggs in strange nests. That lazy cuckoo! I am always quarrelling with her about her conduct. But, good-bye now, little nightingale; it's long past my time for going home. Don't worry yourself, and feel certain that if you are good the world will be a pleasant one for you to live in. Don't be afraid of work. God gives work to all, but one must find pleasure in taking trouble, and birds, alas! have lots to do. It's very, very hard to hatch a good brood, so that all the little ones may be sound and healthy and good." With these words the Goldfinch gave a chirp and disappeared in the air.

"Is what she says true?" thought I. "It may be false. Supposing I were suddenly to begin to trill and jug like my father, and to sing all his songs. Then of course I should not have anything else to do. I should fly about and give concerts, and should I happen to lay an egg I could always put it in a strange nest. What then? The cuckoo does it, and she is very intelligent; she has a charming voice, and she understands that it is far more agreeable to sing songs than to sit whole ages on a nest."

Whilst I was thus reflecting on the sayings of the Goldfinch I was suddenly struck by a noise on the top of a tree, and by the strange words which proceeded from thence. I flew to a fern and perched on the stalk. The words were constantly repeated, " Cuckoo, cuckoo," which means " What a bore!"

"Who can this be," thought I, "who talks about being bored on such a wonderful summer day, and in such a lovely place?"

I looked and looked again on every side, and

at last saw a gray cuckoo; she was perched on a maple bough, and, shaking her head slowly, she was screaming in uniform and dreary tones, "Cuckoo, cuckoo!"

It seemed a pity to me, but I did not dare to speak to her. After screaming thus a number of times she flapped her wings and flew away from the maple tree. But her words still rang in my ears, "Cuckoo" (what a bore)! Her voice still reached me from afar, and it seemed to me that the poor cuckoo could find no pleasant place for herself, although everything about was so beautiful that I could not understand what bored her. Now, if mama were to become thus sorrowful, how I should pity her! and I resolved to watch if mama did so.

On flying to our nest I saw that she was very busy; spreading her wings, she seated my little sisters between them one after the other, teaching them to fly. But it was not at all easy for her, and they did nothing but scream. Mama grew so tired that when she had replaced the last of them in the nest she remained with open beak, breathing hard and almost unable to move a wing. "Poor thing," thought I, "how wearing it must be for her to teach a whole brood to fly! Those stupid children, how tiresome they have grown!" and approaching mama I asked:

"Don't you find those children very wearing?"

"What are you talking about, little birdie? How can I find it wearing to do what will certainly be for your benefit. I am tired, that's all."

"But confess, mama, that all this is simply—"

"Simply what?" asked she.

"A bore," answered I, imitating the cuckoo.

At this mama broke out into a ringing laugh, and, shaking her head, could hardly hold herself up on her tired legs. It seemed laughable even to me when mama said in a stifled voice:

"Oh, you little birdie, how comical you are! I have almost shaken my tuft off with laughing. Fancy your saying that anything is a bore!"

"Do you know, mama, the cuckoo was here during your absence, and spoke only of being bored; so that I felt quite sorry for her, and began to fear that you, also, were bored with your life."

"Don't be uneasy, you little gray thing. You must know that people who look after their business, as I do, have no time even to think of being bored. It's the cuckoo who invented the word; and observe that no bird is so much bored as she; and why, do you think? Because she won't attend to her business, and her only thought is to fly farther and farther away from it. When it is time to have children, then she seeks for strange nests, and lays her eggs there secretly. She is delighted at not having to rear her own children, and doesn't understand how dull it will be for her when she will have nothing to think of but herself. That will really be a bore. Of course, as long as she is young and foolish she finds enjoyment in flying about from the birch tree to the aspen, and from the aspen to the maple; but that soon grows tiresome, and then, if there is no one to love, life soon becomes a burden to every bird. I always pity those poor homeless cuckoos, although they have only themselves to blame. What can be said for them? Youth and folly lead them astray, and then when they have become accustomed to a life of gaiety they can't take to business, and must become bored."

"But, mama, why don't their mothers tell them all this, and teach them to attend to business?"

"You foolish little one, where are their mothers? They never know them, and in a strange nest one can't learn as well as at home. The nurse bird does not even know how to speak to her pupil. Who can teach better than a mother? The thing is out of the question."

"The fact is," thought I to myself, "cuckoos are not nightingales. For if they would only sing as we do, they might really find pleasure in their talent, and yet lay their eggs in strange nests. No, it's quite a different thing for night-ingales."

I longed to sing like my father. I could not bear the thought that I should only be able to whistle like my mother, although that whistle seemed to me at first the most beautiful of songs. But then I was still very small, and understood nothing of music.

Every time my mother flew away in search of food I left the nest and strove hard to sing like my father; but I could not manage it, although I jerked my tail and stuck up my head exactly like him."

I remember one night in particular. The sun had long set, the moon rose over the mere, all the birds were sleeping on the branches. Every-thing around us was peaceful, there was no wind. The trees, the birds, and the grasses kept per-fectly still as if expecting something. The full-blown sweet-brier, the convolvulus, and the clover turned their flowers towards us and seemed to listen. Suddenly, amidst the silence of the night a slight whistling was heard, followed by a rustling in the wood. The birds stirred in their nests, a breeze shook the leaves, all became silent again, and then a wonderful sound was heard, now divided, now united in one sweet note, which spread, died away, and again rang out in the air of the damp night. Hardly did it seem that the glorious singer had exhausted all his art and all his strength, when with fresh brilliancy he burst into a whistle, which sank into a tender and plaintive melody, and ended in a series of clear beats. Thus sang my father.

I was trembling all over with delight, my mother was sitting on a bough as if rooted to the spot, and every living thing in the grove held its breath, listening and listening. When for the last time he had poured forth his harmonious trills, and his last long-drawn note had been repeated by the echo and had died away in the air, I turned my looks downwards. The sweet-brier, inclining its pink flowers, poured large drops of dew on its green leaves, from the edges of the ferns tears trickled into the mere, the white clover blossoms were streaming with dew. The mere trembled and grew pale. But the sky shone all the brighter, and my mother, how happy she felt!

My father sat close to our nest, and, shaking his wings, turned constantly towards her, as if seeking praise from her alone.

From that night I became possessed of the desire to sing like him. Many times afterwards have I spent such a night. But the more the summer advanced the more silent grew my father, whilst mama appeared sadder and quieter. We all observed it. "Mama," asked I at last, "why does papa sing so rarely now, and why are you so sorrowful; has anything happened?"

"No, nothing in particular," answered she with a sigh, "but we are sad because the time for abandoning our dear nests is fast approaching; we shall have to leave them and fly far, far away from our mere."

"Where shall we fly? to Moscow perhaps?" asked I.

"Oh no! Moscow is too near, and it will be cold there as soon as here. We must fly away before the weather becomes worse. Many other birds will fly away like us, but the cranes can wait, they are larger and stronger, and can bear more than we. We are quite different, we must be careful. To-morrow morning, little nightin-gale, we shall assemble near the mere, and take our flight to hot countries."

With these words mama left me.

"To hot countries!" repeated I with extraor-dinary pleasure. "Then we are going at last, and shall see everything—everything! I shall no longer remain at home. Oh how happy I feel! I shall learn to sing like my father, and everything will be so charming,"

The following day we really took to the road.
How astonished I was with everything! To begin
with, after flying a little we came to a house
surrounded with such a quantity of bushes and
flowers that we might all have hidden there.
A number of people were seated on the balcony
of the house; we alighted on one of the bushes
and whistled them a farewell tune. Then all the
people on the balcony turned towards us smiling,
as it seemed, with pleasure, and listening attentively. But we flew on farther, and alighted in
a large garden where there were quantities of
ripe mountain-ash berries. We stopped there,
pecked a little, and then continued our road.

During the first days of our flight we were
very tired and stopped frequently, but afterwards
we became accustomed, and could fly a long
distance in the course of the day. But we
underwent great suffering. Sometimes a pour-
ing rain would assail us on the road, and then
we sought for trees, and hiding beneath them we
pressed close to one another, and awaited the
reappearance of the sun. Sometimes the wind
blew against us, and we had no strength to
resist it; we could not move our wings, and
hardly knew what to do.

At last, after much travelling, we began to
notice that the weather grew milder, the sun

shone more brightly, and storms no longer assailed us on the road. But there were still many hardships and dangers. If it had not been for papa, who flew always in front and showed us the way, I think we should all have perished.

One day we reached a beautiful valley surrounded by very high mountains, and stopped there to rest. Hardly had we settled ourselves on the bough of a large tree than there blew such a cold wind that we all began trembling. On the tops of those mountains lay deep snow and ice, and therefore the wind which blew from them was so fearfully cold we passed the night almost without sleep, pressed close to one another. In the morning, at sunrise, papa dragged us on farther.

Many days had already passed since we left our dear home, and I sometimes remembered mama's words with a sigh. It seemed to me that there we were really happier.

Once, on the banks of a lake, we stopped to spend the night in the ruins of a large castle. We were fearfully fatigued, and at once took up our places for the night, but I saw that my father's mind was ill at ease.

Hardly had we fallen asleep, perched on the cornice of a window and sheltered by thick clusters of ivy, than we heard a fearful scream. Our father hastily aroused us and made us retreat without loss of time, quite under the ivy. Again the cry was heard, and on the walls appeared our terrible enemies the screech-owls. Their eyes shone fearfully as in whole troops they gave chase to any small birds they could find to prey upon.

Oh how frightened we were! Holding our breath we cowered behind the thick layers of ivy, blessing the sombre tinge of our wings, which made us invisible in the semi-darkness. Our enemies screamed several times more with their sinister voices, and then flapping their heavy wings disappeared in the night. We then took to the road and flew away without looking back or stopping, until we had lost sight of the castle, and even of the lake.

From that time forward we tried to stop no longer at night, but to rest in the daytime. All night long we flew onwards and onwards.

"When will our flight come to an end?" asked I one day of mama.

"To-morrow, I trust," answered she, "we shall reach a large garden where the orange trees bloom all through the winter." And, in fact, the following day we reached the garden, where trees with dark green, shiny leaves were covered with beautiful white flowers. Their perfume reached us from afar. 'Twas there we were to live.

But the garden, although very beautiful, did not afford us the same comforts as we enjoyed in our birthplace. Every day we changed our places on the branches, and had no regular residence as in the hazel-tree. There was nowhere to be found in that garden a real thick bush; everything was cleaned and swept, and we longed for grass.

The whole winter we were a prey to anxieties of various kinds. We constantly saw men, and often heard them talking of how pleasant it would be to catch us and place us in a cage.

Then we again changed our place and flew to another garden, where everything was very quiet and the men paid no attention to us. But there we saw before long a cunning cat come climbing up a tree with the intention of seizing us with her cruel claws.

This was all so terrible that we ceased to derive enjoyment from the beautiful weather and wonderful trees of those hot countries. There were none of those bushy thickets such as are to be found in my birthplace; every place was like a garden, with people and dangers everywhere, and the fear of being caught and put in a cage. In the wooded places were found everywhere strange abandoned palaces, around which there grow beautiful and unknown bushes, and such flowers as do not exist at home, as well as rich grass and fresh streams, but in those ruined castles and palaces there always dwelt numbers of owls, and therefore we carefully avoided them.

"Is it possible for us to live any longer in this anxiety?" inquired I of mama; "cannot we find just such another comfortable spot as my birthplace?"

"Do not be uneasy, little nightingale,' answered she. "The time is approaching for us to return home."

I was much surprised and rejoiced.

Very soon afterwards I had a most interesting adventure. One clear, calm night I was perched on an oleander branch, sleeping quietly with my head under my wing. Suddenly the branch on which I was sitting stirred, and close to me rang out a well-known song. I started, turned round, and began listening. The singing was wonderful, but it was not my father's voice. I saw a beautiful gray nightingale seated opposite to me, and singing so sweetly that I had never heard anything like it. I tried to sing to him in my turn, but could only whistle, so that I became confused. Still he was not at all angry; on the contrary, he appeared quite satisfied, and answered my whistle with still louder notes than before.

When the singer had finished he stretched out

his beak towards me and asked me if I loved him and would never leave him.

I answered in surprise, "You cannot know, dear nightingale, that I am unable to sing like you. You would be very sad with me."

"Don't talk nonsense," said he; "your slightest whistle, your smallest feather, are dearer to me than all the world beside. If you will consent to be my wife, I will do everything in my power for you. I will begin by collecting gnats and ants' eggs for your dinner; and when you resolve to love me, we will fly away to a distant land, we will build our nest, and when you sit on the eggs I will sing you every song I know."

I already felt that I loved that dear nightingale, but I could not make up my mind to answer him at once. "What!" thought I; "is it really my fate not to sing at all? am I only to have troubles and worries like poor mama?"

"I thank you, pretty bird, for the proposal," said I at last; "but give me until sunset to-morrow to think it over."

He flew away sadly, and perching on another branch began to sing again, but very gently and plaintively. I pitied him deeply, and felt that I loved him more and more.

The whole of the following day I thought of nothing but him, and by the time it was evening

I understood that I could not live without my dear nightingale. I felt that we must build a nest together in a retired spot free from all danger. The thought was unbearable to me that he should be exposed to danger, and I was far more alarmed on his account than on my own.

When I saw him again and heard the sweet sound of his voice he read at once in my eyes that life without him had no value for me. I now impatiently awaited the day of our flight to my dear country.

We set out on a calm, bright evening, but this time our journey did not appear to me either tiresome or dreadful, because my nightingale was with me and sang me a new song at each resting-place. I was very happy. All that time passed by for me like a beautiful dream, especially on that joyous evening when we just perceived from afar the silvery water of my natal mere, and the lace-like pattern of the opening leaves of the birch tree standing out against the blue sky. We all beat our wings with joy, soaring higher and higher; then, suddenly alighting on the banks of the mere, I at once recognized the hazel bush.

My mother and father flew to a neighbouring bush, whilst I remained with my nightingale amidst the hazel boughs. Regardless of fatigue he sang to me all night, and at sunrise on the following day I began to build my new nest. My husband assisted me by dragging from the mere the heaviest twigs, which I arranged for building, in all haste, a neat and cosy nest.

As soon as it was ready I laid five mottled, greenish eggs, and having surrounded them with soft gray down from my body to keep them warm, I spread out my wings and began sitting.

Everything was in flower about me; the bird-cherry overhung the mere, and at the slightest breeze the white flowers showered their perfumed petals into the water. The gilded fishes moved in shoals through the mere, basking in the sunshine, and from time to time leaping out of the water and falling in again, caused the whole mere to be covered with silvery wavelets. A quantity of glittering gnats whirled through the air or collected in swarms above the trees, whilst troops of cockchafers hummed round the upper boughs. The air was hot and the wood smelt of honey and damp earth, green moss adorned the trees and the hillocks, and in it moved the busy little ants. Everyone was at his own work, and the bees were of course swarming about the bird-cherry and, plunging into the cups of its flowers, extracted from thence their provision of honey.

And he, my dear nightingale—he was perched on a branch near the nest, singing to me of his love, of the beauty of all around, and of the pleasure of sitting near his nest. He taught me with his songs the happiness of being a mother, and the importance of hatching a flourishing brood. I listened with delight, and felt very happy. Only in the evening, at sunset, I went out of the nest and, stretching my benumbed wings, partook of the dinner he had provided. At night I did nothing but listen to the songs of my nightingale.

Thus I sat for twenty days and nights. One bright morning I felt for the first time a slight movement in the nest. I drew carefully on one side, and saw that one of the egg-shells was broken, and that the head of a tiny bird was peeping out of it.

"My own darling little child!" I exclaimed in ecstasy. My nightingale heard my cry and flew to me and looked at our baby. Nothing can ever surpass the happiness of those moments.

One after another our five little bantlings came out of their shells. We threw the shells out of the nest, and I began joyfully to tend and feed my little ones, to love them, and care for their comfort. I had forgotten even to think of singing, I only whistled as well as I could for the amusement of my pets, and they seemed much pleased with the sound.

I was so happy that I began to care more for my neighbours, and sympathized heartily in all their sorrows.

It was just at this time, when I had come to the full enjoyment of my happiness and was tending my children, that I suddenly again heard proceeding from a neighbouring tree the dreary words, "Cuckoo, cuckoo" (a bore, a bore), and with my whole soul I pitied the poor silly cuckoo.

"Deeply and truly is she to be pitied," thought I, and I resolved to record her story on the maple leaves. It may chance that this simple tale of my happy life in my dear, dear home may prove of use to somebody.

THE VIOLET.

THE boisterous autumn wind penetrated roaring and howling into the very heart of the forest. Heavily it struck the slender birches; the withered leaves of the aspen trembled with fear; and the supple willow, bending all her branches downward, shed bitter tears on the bosom of the blue terror-stricken lake. The fir stood upright gazing into the hazy sky, all his needles erect with alarm; whilst the trunks of the young birches turned paler than ever with anxiety. The wind blew roughly, tearing away the last dry leaves; forcibly separated from their parent branches, they whirled through the air, heedless, through dismay and terror, where the wind might drop them at last; hurled and whirled in disorder through the atmosphere, they crumbled and fell powerless to the ground. The oak alone stood unmoved, driving his sturdy roots deep into the ground; his thick and vigorous trunk clung firmly to the soil, and, sending out in all directions his crooked boughs, he calmly withstood the violence of the wind. His yellow leaves stuck in knots to the branches, and, closely linked together, would not suffer the wind to sever them from their parent stem. "When the time comes we shall fall of our own accord," said they; "the wind sha'n't tear us off by force, that it sha'n't." The wood was full of disorder and tumult. The earth was covered with dried-up branches and strewn with sere and yellow leaves.

At the foot of the mighty oak crouched, hardly to be observed, a tiny dried-up violet. The little plant was entirely withered, its dry leaves had curled themselves up and murmured pitifully to one another. The head of the long-since faded flower hung downwards, and her pallid face bore the traces of tears.

The wind having sufficiently devastated the summits of the trees, turned downwards and rushed with cruel violence along the ground as if it wished to sweep away the crumbling soil. Two more leaves were rent from the violet and whirled powerless to meet their severed comrades. The faded flower leant against the root of the oak. "I am dying," she murmured; "farewell God's universe!"

But the wind ceased; it swept away, leaving

the desolated wood in peace at last. Overcome
with terror the violet still rested her frail head
on the oak's root. Everything was quiet in the
wood, faint moans alone were heard in all directions. The violet raised her eyes timidly; she
recalled all her youth: the spring, the caressing
sunbeams, the warm spring showers, the beauty
of her green leaves, the short summer nights
when she listened entranced to the song of the
nightingale, and the pink light of the dewy morn.
She remembered it all with bitter regret.

"Farewell, old oak!" she murmured pitifully.
"I thank you for your shade and coolness; you
have been kind to me, every one has been kind,
and I thank every one. Farewell, God's world!
I have loved you so passionately, and have been
so happy; but all is finished for me now, I am
dying."

The old oak, who disdained to bend to the
violence of the wind, now bowed his head downwards and looked in the direction of his feet.
"You are suffering, little violet," said he; "though
the wind shake us, though the rain beat against
us, and the snow crush down our branches, we
shall not die."

"But my heart has already nearly ceased to
beat, the sap no longer runs through my veins, I
feel the approach of death," said the violet in a

feeble voice. "Do not deceive me, old oak, I know that I am dying."

"No one dies out of the world," replied the oak triumphantly. "When I first sprang up in this wood, before me lay the seeds of all those that grow round us. I have seen their childhood and their youth, I have seen much in my time, and have thought many deep thoughts; nothing dies altogether, believe me, young violet."

These words impressed the violet, and a ray of hope found its way to her agonized soul.

"Continue talking to me, old oak," she said in a failing voice; "your words comfort me."

The oak was silent and reflected awhile. "Listen," he continued. "Once I saw a young birch-tree die. In those days I was young myself. I loved the poor flexible tree, and could not bear to see her sufferings; my heart bled for her. She grew in freedom near me, well proportioned and white as snow; wondrously waved her slender branches in the spring breezes, wondrous were the perfumes her leaves gave forth in the calm luminous nights. The little birch-tree was gay and happy, but a man came and slew the young tree. He tore off her white bark and stripped her delicate frame. The sap ran in red streams from her wounds. I saw how her leaves withered and curled, I saw her grow sad and die slowly.

" The spring came, her leaves remained folded, her slender dry branches began to break off, at last the flexible trunk itself leant over to one side, and each day bent nearer to the ground."

" One summer morning I heard a cracking sound. I looked, and had barely time to stretch out my wide-spreading arms when the poor little tree fell straight upon my breast. I remained stupefied with sorrow, holding her firmly in my embrace.

" I know not how long I remained gazing down at her in deep despair. It seems that many days and nights must have flown over my head. When I awoke my trunk was covered with gray moss.

" Life seemed very hard to bear then, but time did not stand still, and my precious burden began to crumble away on my breast. My life grew wearisome to me, and for a long time I seemed to care for nobody."

" How did it come to pass? It was, as I now remember, spring; life regained its own; I felt new energies awake in my trunk. I looked around me, glancing at the spot where my vanished one had been; my heart beat violently. There, in the very same place, I saw a slender young birch-tree resembling my beloved in every feature. I stretched out my boughs and tossed my head, thinking it was a dream. But it was not a dream; my little birch-tree stood on sound roots, not a worm had reached her heart, she was pure and untainted, and was now throwing out fresh shoots still more beautiful than her former growth.

"Nothing dies altogether; believe and hope," concluded the old oak, looking up to the sky; whilst the leaves at his summit fluttered, and his head nodded cheerily.

Closely the violet pressed her head against the roots of the old oak-tree; her strength was leaving her, but her heart was possessed by a consoling feeling, "Is it possible," thought she, "that all is not ended for me?" She thought of her roots; "has no wicked worm penetrated to my heart?"—the thought agitated her—"but no, the soil round the oak is healthy, my roots are sound and cool, I have always preserved them. Is it possible that all be not ended?" Her heart beat painfully.

"Let it be with me as with the young birch-tree," whispered she. "I leave all to the Unseen Power which can work miracles; oh, beloved nature, save me!" she exclaimed for the last time, and sank into a deep sleep.

The wind roared much after this; it broke the dry branches and bent the flexible plants. Winter came, and covered the earth with a thick white mantle. The birch boughs bent and crackled beneath its weight. Dully groaned the old oak, but firmly he stood, clinging fast to the earth with his mighty roots. A tiny hillock of frozen snow indicated the spot where the violet had been, no other sign of her was left; the cruel frost chained everything; the trees bore its fetters in silence, their naked boughs alone stretched upwards towards the blue sky as if to pray for strength. The red sun, from time to time, cast a stolen glance at his dear ones, he arose in the sky, slipped sideways between the branches, kissed the naked brows of the trees in passing, and again played stealthily with the frozen drops on the boughs; then with slow and noiseless steps he glided away from the wood, and was hidden behind the edge of the globe. For a long time he did not reappear, and the inhabitants of the wood began to despair; but the sun did not suffer them to be entirely cast down. Shining out stealthily from behind the clouds he glanced at the wood and said, "Hope." That one word revived their strength, they all became cheerful and waited in silence. "When, oh when! come quickly, red sun!" rustled a young willow, and all the branches of the wood repeated her words, producing a light ringing sound. Then the young willow bent over the frozen mere, and tried with her stiffened boughs whether the transparent ice would not give way. The sun shone forth again and again disappeared, the frozen droplets reflecting his smile. The snow glistened in diamond stars, the old oak seemed to grow young again in the rosy light, the whole scene glowed and flushed, but after a minute all was again pale and deathlike.

But now the winter is past; the red sun strikes oftener and oftener upon field and meadow, and no longer stealthily and hurriedly, but long and gaily he plays with the streams of water which pour from every branch. The snow ceases to hold out, but grows softer, and longs already to melt into water; but the frost will not yet give way to the sun, and when the latter sinks beneath the horizon he is there again. He stops the flowing streams, freezes the softening snow, and arrests the sap in the branches. Every day the sun remains absent for a shorter time, and at last he completely overcomes the frost.

The white snow is no longer in the wood; the branches of the trees are freed from it, and stretch themselves languidly; the red sap runs gaily through them, the earth awakes from its deep sleep and basks in the red sunshine. Here and there green moss grows up, and whole families of young grasses thrust forth their thick, reddish heads. The old oak is full of enjoyment, he shakes off his yellow leaves, and begins to deck himself with a fresh green foliage. He adorns and purifies himself; he casts a glance on the ground at his feet; the young violet is already dressed out in her little dark green leaves, they are so numerous that she can hardly show her tiny head; but lo! she has succeeded, though her eyes are still closed and her face is enveloped in a fine green veil. The old oak looks on and admires. Little by little the veil gives way, at last it falls back upon her shoulders, her folded leaves spread themselves out, her happy eyes open and she looks about her, she turns round to her neighbours, and then upwards to the sky; folding crosswise two of her green leaves, she sends up a faint cloud of wondrous fragrance.

"Good morning, kind old oak," she cries with a joyous nod.

"Your heart was pure and untainted and you have revived," said the old oak. And he who scorned to bow to the storm bent low to the modest violet.

THE PIGEON.

ENEATH the high roof of an old country house lived a colony of pigeons. There was a large number of them, all gray with little red legs. Amongst them lived a single snow-white pigeon with a tufted head and pink legs covered with downy white stockings. Her large round eyes shone with a bright and wondrously tender light. She always perched on the highest corner of the barn or walked along its edge, recalling by her soft cooing the murmur of water running in a shallow stream, amidst shining pebbles.

All the gray pigeons knew and loved her; nor was this strange, she was so good and gentle.

One summer morning the white pigeon came out of the roof by the barn window and sat upon the ledge, looking about her with her soft brilliant eyes.

It was a delightful morning, not a cloud in the sky; the tall trees were motionless, their tops

standing out clearly defined against the blue
sky.   The white pigeon, having looked at everything which could be seen near her, stretching
out her downy neck and moving her tufted head,
began to coo.

"Live in peace! live in peace!" the voice rose
higher and higher, but her gray companions did
not notice her.

They were already accustomed to these words
and quite agreed with them.

Suddenly the pigeon stopped; at the top of
the garret a terrible scuffling and screaming was
heard.   She listened and looked up: it was caused
by two sparrows.   They were quarrelling violently and flying at one another, and as they
both screamed at once it was difficult to ascertain
the cause of the dispute.

It should be known that both the screamers
were very small; one of them was called Graywing, and the other Ruffler.

What could two such tiny creatures find to
get angry about? Ruffler was fluttering about
with a threatening air, and screaming with all
his strength.

"You're a fool! you're a fool! you know nothing."

"No, you're a fool!" retorted Graywing with
still more violence.

"Not at all," furiously interrupted Ruffler. "You don't know, and I do. Tell me, then, which are the most numerous, the stars in the sky or the flowers in the fields?"

"You idiot!" twittered Graywing; "who doesn't know that! Of course the flowers are the most numerous; why, even the cherries in the garden are more numerous."

"Not at all, that's a falsehood," screamed Ruffler with his feathers all awry; "the stars are most numerous, I have seen it myself."

"No! the flowers and cherries are more numerous."

"No! the stars."

"No! the cherries."

The screaming became fearful. "Live in peace live in peace!" was heard from the barn window but the disputants listened to nothing, they shrieked with all their strength, and were on the point of coming to blows.

Suddenly a jackdaw arrived to the rescue. He alighted on the barn window, and, flapping his wings, croaked so hoarsely that the sparrows were frightened and became silent. The cooing was then heard distinctly: "Live in peace!" the sparrows heard it, and looked down in confusion.

The Jackdaw croaked scornfully.

"What a folly that peacemaking is!" said he

mockingly. "Don't hear her, gentlemen," continued he to the sparrows. "I am much interested in your discussion; and that twaddling white pigeon is so extraordinarily dull that she has been repeating the same thing for the last century, without considering that youth aspires towards knowledge and truth; why, that's as it should be. I know the world, I've lived amongst men, I have learnt much, and have myself become so wondrously wise that they have fastened this piece of red cloth to my neck as a sign of my learning. Here it is, you can look at it!" and the jackdaw pointed with dignity to a piece of rag which was hanging from his neck.

The young sparrows felt full of timidity and confusion.

"I'll tell you what it is, gentlemen," continued the jackdaw; "you have really a most learned subject for discussion, and here is the best way of settling it. Let the respectable Mr. Ruffler count all the stars in the sky, while young Mr. Graywing prepares a correct account of all the flowers and cherries. That's how men manage it. I know all about it. When the poultry-wife, Matrona, wishes to know how many chickens and ducklings she has she at once counts them."

Here the jackdaw stopped suddenly, as if some disagreeable scene had recurred to him. "And now, good-bye, gentleman," said he; "really I must be off; they are waiting for me down there, and men must not be kept waiting. I believe they have already prepared some food for me— they might become alarmed lest I should have left them altogether. You see, I live in a golden cage, I eat of the best, and every one listens to me as soon as I open my mouth."

The jackdaw croaked and flapped his heavy wings.

The sparrows looked at each other and strutted about.

"Well, then," said Ruffler with dignity, "I have nothing to say against it. Science is science. I will reckon the stars, and will meet you to-morrow at this very spot."

"Agreed!" answered Graywing with much gravity. "I'll do the same for the flowers and cherries."

"Live in peace!" was heard from the window where the pigeon sat.

But the sparrows in flying downwards flew purposely against her beak as if by accident.

The white pigeon turned a soft glance upon them, looked around her with her brilliant eyes, and flew into the barn.

Graywing flew straight to the fields and, sitting on a fence, set to counting the flowers. He had hardly got to the middle of the meadow when his head began to turn.

"How is this? I shall never finish this account. It is fearful what a quantity of flowers there are, they've bored me already. I had better go and see if I sha'n't succeed more easily with the cherries."

He then flew across the fence, and, seated on a cherry-tree, began to count its fruit. But they were so ripe that several of them had burst open, and their juice was oozing out in dark drops.

Graywing thought he had better dine. After eating some cherries he began to feel unusually heavy about the crop and exceedingly idle.

"What nonsense all this is, to be sure!" said he. "I am certain that the flowers and the cherries are the most numerous. Such is my conviction. And to have to count them all the same, what trouble! No, I'll say I have counted them, and there's an end of it."

So Graywing flew away to the kitchen-garden to see what the cabbages were doing.

Meanwhile Ruffler was awaiting the evening, firmly resolved to count every star in the firmament.

"Yes, I'll do it," thought he, "and prove that I'm right. I won't sleep all night. I'll number every star in the sky. I'll sit on the top of the balcony which looks out on the large square; there is an open space in front, and I shall see everything."

No sooner said than done. Ruffler perched on the top of the balcony as soon as it began to get dark, and commenced operations. For each fresh star he gave a hop on his slender legs; but they soon began to overspread the sky in such numbers that the sagacious Ruffler had hardly time to wag his tail before a fresh cluster of diamonds shone out in the dark-blue sky.

In the midst of the sky appeared a transparent milky river, flowing and sparkling from end to end with innumerable twinkling stars.

Ruffler stared with dazzled eyes from side to side. It was the first time he had ever looked upon such an endless multitude of stars, for he was generally asleep directly after sunset. He gazed at them with all his might, quite forgetting to count, under the influence of an unknown pleasure.

Suddenly was heard resounding through the calm, starry night, "Live in peace!" and for the moment an unwonted feeling stole over Ruffler.

"That white pigeon is not so silly after all. What has come over me?" screamed he harshly directly afterwards; "am I also becoming a simpleton? I have scientific views, how can I attend to such twaddle? It must be the effect of drowsiness—it is really time to sleep. It is clear that the stars are more numerous than the cherries."

With these words he flew to a lilac bush, tucked his head under his wing, and fell asleep.

Early in the morning the two quarrelsome sparrows met on the roof. The jackdaw was already there anxiously expecting the scientific debate.

"Well, then," said he, "have you collected the necessary information, gentlemen?"

"I have counted all the flowers and cherries," boasted Graywing. "Their number is so great that it could not be written down from here to the end of the barn. What can there be to dispute about that?"

"And I saw so many stars," answered Ruffler, "that I grew tired of counting them, and gave it up; the more so that no one can count them; it is useless to try. And suppose them even to be counted, you couldn't write down their number on four acres of ground. Such are the facts, and there's nothing more to be said on the subject."

"That there is," screamed quarrelsome Graywing. "You're a fool! and the flowers and cherries are so much the more numerous that you dare not dispute any longer."

"You're a fool!" answered Ruffler contemptuously, "and I don't want to talk with you."

"Now, then, gentlemen," interposed the crow, "the figures are of no importance; you can perfectly discuss without them. A well-bred sparrow should firmly maintain his own opinion; and if you are certain, there can be no mistake about the matter."

"Without doubt," vociferated the sparrows.

"Now, that is what men call a conviction," said the jackdaw with a knowing look; "and when that is the case a learned man cannot and ought not to give way."

Adopting this view, the two sparrows hopped fiercely at one another.

"Away with figures and accounts!" screamed they.

"I stick to my opinion," said Ruffler warmly.

"And I'll never give way," said Graywing.

"I'm convinced that I'm right."

"And I'm convinced that you're a fool."

"That's right, gentlemen, that's right," screamed the jackdaw; "keep to your own opinions. Bravo! Br-r-ravo!! Hoorray!!!

He feared that the dispute would not be prolonged, and wished extremely to lead the two sparrows to a fight.

Nor had the jackdaw long to wait. The two adversaries, tired of tearing their throats with screaming, rushed at one another. Ruffler pecked Graywing in the eye, and Graywing clutched and tore off his opponent's top-knot. The combat was a tremendous one.

"Live in peace!" resounded from the barn.

The jackdaw was flapping his wings with delight as he hopped deftly on one side when the combatants came unpleasantly near. The roof was already wet with blood, but the jackdaw continued screaming, "Br-r-ravo! br-r-ravo! give it him! tear him!"

But the sparrows were already past all hearing. They thought only of injuring one another, and, linked closely together, they rolled in one ball along the side of the roof, whence they would have fallen and been shattered to atoms if a ledge of wood nailed to the sill of the barn window had not arrested their downward progress.

They both fell senseless at the feet of the white pigeon.

Shrinking slightly from them she turned aside her brilliant eyes, which were wet with tears; and, with a soft movement of her wings, drew the lifeless sparrows within the barn window, where there was a large heap of wool. They rolled down upon it and lay for a long time without the slightest motion of their tiny wings.

The pigeon smoothed the wool with her gentle beak, seated herself close to them, and awaited their recovery.

The sparrows lay thus for a long time; but the coolness of the barn, and a fresh breeze blowing in at the window, awoke them at last. Ruffler was the first to open his eyes.

The stars already began to appear in the sky, and through the triangular window a complete sheaf of diamonds was visible. All was quiet.

Ruffler raised his head, and the memory of the preceding night at once returned to him.

"Live in peace!" reached his ears from below.

He closed his eyes and listened attentively. Graywing also recovered his senses, and, gazing at the sheafs of diamonds, he listened to the pigeon's cooing and reflected. How clear and soft it sounded in the calmness of the night! The stars twinkled in silence, the placid trees whispered together, whilst the flowers slept in the plain. All things told of peace and happiness.

Suddenly from the opposite barn window was heard the furious croaking of the jackdaw.

"Murder!" screamed he; "help! police!"

The pigeon looked in that direction and saw that the poultry-wife, Matrona, had fastened the jackdaw with a dirty rag to a pole which was fixed on the roof of the poultry shed.

"I have caught you at last, you scoundrel," screamed Matrona; "you'll slip away from me again, won't you? you robber! Oh, yes, of course you'll break loose! You'll get no more chickens to smother, no more ducklings to strangle, that I promise you, my dear little dove."

With these words Matrona securely fastened the neck of the luckless old jackdaw to the pole with the dirty rag.

The sparrows looked on in amazement.

The starry sky shone with unclouded brilliancy. The pale moon looked caressingly into the barn, and the white pigeon cooed:

"Live in peace!"

The sparrows drew close to her and pressed themselves to her downy wings. They were ashamed to look at one another.

"How glorious the sky is!" said Graywing at last.

"And so is the earth," answered Ruffler.

"Yes," cooed the pigeon, "live in peace!" and all was silence.

THE BUTTERFLY.

HOW pleasant it was on the large burdock leaf on the evening when this history begins. It must be admitted that one seldom sees such a ball. The butterfly was keeping her birthday. That very morning she awoke from her long sleep, and, bursting the shell of her chrysalis, appeared in the form of a charming blue butterfly. Her wings were of velvet, from her head sprang two golden feelers of the finest shape, and her waist was inclosed in a dark velvet bodíce.

But freshly delivered from her narrow cell she knew not her own beauty, but only wondered at the glory of God's world, and remembered that it had once before been known to her.

As she moved in this mood along the thick burdock leaf she felt a strong desire to drink; continuing her way to where a hollow, which ran the whole length of the large veins, had collected so much water as to form a deep canal, she bent

F

her head to satisfy her thirst, when she suddenly saw before her the reflection of her own image.

Goodness, how pretty I am! thought the butterfly, keeping her eyes on the water; and turning round she unfolded her wings and examined herself on every side; her heart beat with joy, but she was alone on the leaf and could speak of it to no one.

'Twas then that the idea of giving a ball, and inviting her neighbours to keep her birthday, first arose in her mind. With this purpose she carefully examined the leaf, in the hope of discovering some other inhabitants on it.

And in truth, from the reverse of the thick leaf a most extraordinary noise was heard, and looking in that direction she saw a big gray spider working heartily to strengthen a large, round, star-like web, to which the fluffy reverse of the burdock served as a roof. He was so much occupied that he did not observe the coming of his elegant visitress.

"I beg your pardon," said the butterfly, stopping short. "I don't know your name," she added, with embarrassment.

"Spider," was the hurried answer, without any interruption to the work.

"Now the fact is," continued the butterfly, "I

wanted to ask you to come to me this evening. This is my birthday, and I wish to get up a small party. If you will honour me I shall be very happy; I live on the other side of this leaf."

"I'll be there," answered the spider as hurriedly as before; "that is to say, if I finish my work before the evening," added he, climbing up his web.

The butterfly, slightly astonished, returned to the other side of the leaf; there she stopped and began to reflect.

"Well," thought she, "if all my guests are as unsociable as this one I sha'n't derive much pleasure from their company."

She was standing on the very edge of the leaf, whence hung a large drop of dew ready to fall to the ground; it was perfectly transparent, and reflected the butterfly's image. She could not desist from admiring herself, and thought that, after all, her party would be a very gay one. Extending her delicate wings, she flew from the leaf to a clump of grass, and alighted in the midst of a complete assembly collected round a grasshopper, who was giving a concert on the fiddle; a number of ants, beetles, lady-birds, flies, and gnats were moving about him.

At the sudden appearance of the graceful

butterfly the attention of every one was turned to her, and a murmur of approbation arose from all sides.

"How charming, how beautiful!" they cried with one voice. The grasshopper threw down his fiddle, quite overcome with delight.

The butterfly was much pleased, though the attention of the numerous assembly confused her. Bending her neck modestly, and folding back her wings, she made her way to a large blue fly, and with a graceful curtsy and timid voice she murmured:

"Excuse me, madam, if I disturb you. I am afraid I have interrupted—"

"Not at all, my pretty one, no interruption whatsoever; your coming has most agreeably surprised us. But where do you come from? Nobody knows you here."

"I am still very young," answered the butterfly timidly. "I am unacquainted with the neighbourhood, and did not, therefore, expect to come upon so numerous an assembly."

"I am the mistress here, and my name is Blue-bottle," answered the other. "Delighted to make your acquaintance. Make yourself at home, I beg you, quite without ceremony."

"Since such is the case, may I ask you to attend my birthday party?" said the butterfly in a low voice. "I am giving a small party on the burdock leaf yonder."

"For my part, I shall be most happy," said the fly with a bow. "Why shouldn't I visit you? I don't stand on my dignity, I call on every one."

"Will you come too? and you, and you?" said the butterfly, addressing each of the company in turn, with a graceful bow.

All expressed their willingness to be present, and the grasshopper in particular felt so pleased that he couldn't keep his seat, but showed his delight by a series of hops, although he felt it was not quite proper on so slight an acquaintanceship. But he couldn't help it; his joy and his sorrow were both expressed by skips; every one knew it, and thought nothing of it.

On her return home the butterfly felt very hungry, and seeing close to her burdock a sweet-brier bush, she flew to it, and began sucking the delicate juice from the yellow heart of the flower. The bush was already occupied by a handsome bee, who was diligently occupied in collecting the sweet and perfumed honey.

"Here's another guest," thought the butterfly as she flew over to her and offered her an invitation.

"Very well, my darling," answered the bee with a busy air; "if I can manage to get through my work, I'll certainly come. You see we're a busy set, and have no time to enjoy ourselves; but one must make exceptions sometimes, and you're such a darling that I should like to make your acquaintance."

The bee flew away heavily laden with honey, and the butterfly ate what she had left.

But it was time to get ready for the ball. The heat had already diminished, and the air was growing cool. Everything was ready at the appointed time, the burdock leaf neatly arranged, and a carpet of rosy leaves culled from the neighbouring bush was spread upon the floor.

"The blue-bottle will certainly not dance, she is so stout, and, I suppose, no longer young. The spider won't dance either; so I'll prepare a place for them here, where they can talk together."

The butterfly awaited her guests with impatience. She felt a strong desire to dance and chat. Seeing everything was in order, she began to arrange herself, with the dewdrop for a mirror, and to try the skill of her legs and wings.

At last the guests began to assemble. The blue-bottle was the first to arrive, and the young mistress of the house could then examine her at her ease. The fly was very glossy, her wings glistened with bright-blue tints in the light of the setting sun. In spite of her venerable appearance she looked at herself in the looking-glass, and raising her forelegs she sleeked her head and face several times with them. The grasshopper tuned his fiddle and began to play a valse. The gnats were the first to flutter through the air; they were followed by the blue fly, who struck the floor heavily in her flight; then came the mistress of the house, who, extending her delicate wings, rose into the air and began to turn with a rapidity at which she was herself astonished.

The party was a gay one; all the guests circled and wheeled to the music of the grasshopper, who played without ceasing, whilst they agreed with one voice that the evening was a delightful one.

Meanwhile the sun had set, and the weary company seated itself upon the leaf to rest.

Suddenly the forgotten and dusty spider made his appearance. He advanced to the butterfly, and, extending his leg gracefully, begged to be excused for his late arrival. He had only just finished his work. "Never mind," said the butterfly; "I am only sorry you were not here to enjoy yourself with us. And now, shall we all go to supper?"

The company rose from their places, the but-

terfly leading the way, and, climbing up the red
stem of the sweet-brier, all the guests collected
on it.   The supper was laid on a thick branch on
which five fine flowers had freshly opened; each
of them was lighted up by a bright glowworm;
the light was very brilliant.   From the small,
hanging dewdrops innumerable rays were reflected, so that the whole branch shone from afar
as if covered with diamonds.   The butterfly
pressed her guests to taste the sweet honey, the
fresh dew, and the perfumed juice of the flowers.
When they were all seated she began searching
for the blue-bottle, but to her great surprise she
saw her in the distance, flying away with a
vicious buzz, so that she soon lost sight of her.
This conduct much annoyed and astonished the
butterfly; but the ball continued its course, and
the supper was thought magnificent, though
everyone did not enjoy the entertainment equally.
The ants sat on one side and sulked, the spider
occasionally squinted in the direction where the
blue-bottle had vanished; but the lady of the
house did not observe these details, and feeling
hungry sipped the sweet and refreshing food
with great satisfaction.   She thought it very jolly.

On taking leave all the guests expressed their
thanks to her, and the gnats, in particular, were
so pleased and delighted that they knew not how

sufficiently to praise her beautiful party. But as everything must come to an end, this charming evening finished at last, and the guests went off to sleep. A few of the glowworms alone continued to light up the rosy precincts where the supper had been laid, and the dew glistened as at first, illuminating each little leaf.

The grasshopper, after the ball, sank down upon the grass exhausted, and fell into a profound sleep; but still in his dreams he saw the beautiful butterfly and her delightful ball, and half waking seized his fiddle and ran the bow once or twice over the strings, and then all was silence again.

The leaf on which the weary butterfly slept moved gently in the evening breeze, and the sweet-brier strewed the burdock with a shower of rosy petals.

The butterfly slept soundly all night, and only awoke when the spider at work on his web began to beat violently against the floor. Perhaps something is wrong with him, thought she, flying hastily to the edge of the leaf.

" What has happened, neighbour?" asked she, bending her feelers towards him.

" Nothing," returned he.

" I fancied there was something unusual," lisped the butterfly, "I heard such a noise."

"Nothing but work," returned the spider, not quite pleased. "There'll be rain this evening, and I must arrange my web."

"Well, then," asked the butterfly timidly, "what did you think of my yesterday's ball?"

"Very good, there's nothing to be said, everything was arranged with taste; and as for the company, well—there was only—"

"But what was there bad in the company?" asked the butterfly in surprise.

"Well, the company was all good; there was only that fly, the blue one. If I could only catch her in my web—if she were to fall into it. Now, let me advise you, neighbour, to avoid her acquaintance; you're very young, and she's very wicked and stupid."

The butterfly looked at him pettishly, and thought to herself: "How cross he is to-day! He must be in a bad humour; it's best to be off as quick as possible;" and she climbed gently up to her leaf.

"Now I must go and see the world. I shall spend the whole day in visiting and looking at everything, to learn how people live and what their occupations are."

She rose high in the air to try her wings, and finding them sufficiently strong she flew with joy to a variegated meadow, alighting on the flowers on her road, and thinking with compassion of her cross neighbour and his unfinished web, so gray and so ugly. "What an idea!" thought she; "on such a marvellous day to work at so sad an occupation!"

She flew about all day without fatigue, and already began to think of not returning home for the night, but of spending it simply and rurally in the cup of a many-leaved, double poppy.

Whilst our beauty sat reflecting on her foregone enjoyment, reclining without one thought of anxiety on a slender stalk of basil, there blew a sudden gust of wind. The whole meadow was agitated, and the flowers bent their beautiful heads to the ground. The poor butterfly was so shaken that she fell suddenly from her couch, a cloud of golden dust indicating the track of her fall. Poor thing, how terrified she was! She could hardly manage to rise again, limping, and with a violent pain in her slender back.

But there was no time to be lost. She must fly home at once to the stout burdock leaf, which would certainly protect her from the bad weather. With an effort she rose and flew off at once, sinking from time to time upon the grass, and feeling every minute that her strength was leaving her. With great trouble she reached her home, and sank half fainting on the edge of the leaf.

But, alas! her misfortunes were not yet ended. Rain began to fall in heavy drops. It struck so violently upon her velvety back that she could only run about the leaf trembling with fear and reft of the strength to unfold her wings saturated with damp. Death seemed already near to her, and her thoughts were wandering to her gay companions, when suddenly on the border of the leaf the spider appeared.

"Come quick to me," exclaimed be, out of breath; "the rain will beat you to death."

With what joy did she follow him; and how great was her surprise to find on entering his thick web that not one drop of rain penetrated into the spider's house! The room was dark but completely dry, and it held so firmly to the fluffy reverse of the leaf that the wind could hardly penetrate it.

Oh how pleasant it seemed to the poor butter-fly to be there, and how warmly she thanked her deliverer! Tears ran down her cheeks as she trembled from the effects of her recent fears. The spider was indeed very kind, but his ungainly manners, his rough clothes, and dusty appearance had at first frightened the poor little thing. She now clearly understood that it was very fortunate for her to have such a neighbour.

"Listen. to me, child," said the spider. "I am

old enough to talk to you as to a daughter. I am aware of your inexperience, but you are a dear, good, little neighbour, and I want to give you a piece of useful advice. I see that the praise of your new acquaintances has completely turned your head; nor is that wonderful, you are really very charming. But just understand this, don't listen to the advice and silly opinions of the blue-bottle."

"But why?" asked the astonished butterfly. "She is always so good to me, and no later than yesterday she took me with her to see the world."

"Just so," cried the spider; "that's exactly what I expected, she has already been working upon you with her rubbish. Hasn't she taken you to some house or other where men live?"

The butterfly became embarrassed and surprised. Who could have told the spider of it? It was just as he had said. In the morning the fly had met her, and had pressed her strongly to fly with her to a place where she would see things she had never even dreamt of before.

"I am surprised at that fly," continued the spider, firing up. "Not only won't she stay at home herself, but she must mislead others. What! live without society! impossible!" said the spider, mimicking the fly.

"But what am I to do?" asked the butterfly,

quite upset. "I have already given my word."

"Well, you know best," answered the spider. "My duty is to warn you; but you are not too young to judge, and consider for yourself; I won't detain you."

And he climbed up the side of his web. The rain had ceased, the sun shone brightly, and they both went out into the open world.

"Just look now," said the spider.

The butterfly obeyed, and opened her eyes with wonder. How beautiful it was! The star-like web was besprinkled with rain, its innumerable threads were decked with tiny dewdrops which shone like precious stones, the sun played upon each of them in turn until the whole web resembled a magnificent star composed of rings of diamonds.

"How beautiful!" cried the butterfly in ecstasies.

"Yes, you foolish one, everything is gold that glitters for you. If you had to dry it now. Ah! what a life ours is!" and he shuffled back into his house.

The butterfly did not sleep all that night. She could not get rid of the thought of her trials and sufferings, and the spider's words haunted her little brain.

"What am I to do not to quarrel with him?"

thought she. She longed so to see the world. " No, I won't go," resolved she. " The spider has not warned me in vain. He is sure to be right. I'll slip out in quite a different direction to avoid the fly, and come back again at night. No, I positively won't go. I might have to undergo the same sufferings there as when that terrible wind was blowing."

So saying she fixed herself firmly to the leaf, and having made a strong resolution not to listen to the fly she fell peacefully asleep.

The morning came, the weather was beautiful. After the rain the flowers looked gayer and brighter than ever, and their sweet juice stood in large drops upon their petals. On all sides a humming was heard; swarms of bees were engaged in collecting honey, and the gnats were whirling round in the air. The butterfly awoke late, and gazing on the brilliant sun smiled at the trouble of the past day. She saw in every pool of water collected on the leaves the reflection of her own image, and felt full of joy. Her back no longer gave her pain, her bodice glistened in the sun, and her feelers were tinged with golden hues. " What nonsense!" thought she. " Last night I was so much shaken that everything seemed terrible. Whatever may be said, God's world is very beautiful."

She did not, however, abandon her intention of avoiding the fly, and was already preparing to take flight for that purpose. Hardly, however, had she alighted on some neighbouring honey-suckles to get her breakfast, when the blue-bottle unexpectedly arrived there.

The butterfly's heart beat violently, and she pretended not to see her. But that was not to be. The fly had been on the look-out for her, and had observed her on the bush when she flew up to her and began buzzing into her ear.

"Listen to me, darling; I've been longing for you. Let us start as it was arranged. They expect us there already."

The butterfly did not answer, and tried to get away on the opposite side; but the fly would not leave her, and continued whispering in her ear:

"It will be gayer there than you can even imagine. You will laugh at your own ball with your sweet-briers and glowworms. One candle will give more light than all your glowworms."

By this time the butterfly no longer resisted, but listened attentively.

"And as I am already invited," went on buzz-ing the fly, "and as I promised to bring you with me, mind you are ready; I'll call for you myself." And with these words the blue-bottle flew away.

The curiosity of the butterfly was violently

excited. " What! is it possible that there should be a ball finer than ours on the burdock? I don't think that can be the case; nothing like it was ever seen. Can she be speaking falsely? I am fearfully anxious to know."

And the unfortunate butterfly remained irresolute.

Meanwhile in a rich country house preparations for a large ball were being made. Everything there was in motion. The men-servants were arranging the rooms, the pretty mistress with her daughters was filling large crystal bowls with fruits, the chamber-maids were driving out the flies, the children were bringing in from the garden and fields quantities of flowers and disposing them in large nosegays on the tables, one bouquet of field-flowers ornamented the centre of the drawing-room table. When all was ready a number of candles were lighted and the guests made their appearance.

Conversation, laughter, and music united in one general murmur. In the dancing-hall and drawing-room all the windows looking on the garden were still shut. It soon, however, became impossible to breathe, and a little girl ran to the balcony door and threw it wide open; at the same moment a slight buzzing was heard, and in flew the blue-bottle with the beautiful blue butterfly behind her. The glitter and noise overcame the butterfly so completely, that she stopped at once and alighted on the top of the door. But the indefatigable fly hurried her onwards. "Now, then, don't be shy, you silly thing," she buzzed. "It is quite a shame to see such countrified manners. What are you stopping for?"

"It seems so dreadful to me," whispered the butterfly.

"What nonsense!" mocked the fly; "she's found something terrible to be afraid of. There, go to your friends; there's your beloved sweet-brier, and your honeysuckle, and all that rubbish."

When the butterfly saw the beautiful nosegay she became somewhat livelier and alighted on it timidly. "A butterfly, a butterfly! such a pretty one, come and see!" screamed a little girl who was standing near the table.

Two young girls advanced to the bouquet and began to admire her. Their praises completely turned our beauty's head. She climbed up the flowers, and, to be the better seen, began fluttering about them, whilst the fly still buzzed. "Nearer to the light, nearer, you silly country girl; the company is admiring you, and you won't take a step to show yourself." Timidly the butterfly approached the candles and commenced flying in wide circles round them, but soon her head became giddy, her heart began to palpitate, the circle grew narrower, until at last, flying straight into the candle, she felt a burning pain and fell senseless in the centre of the nosegay. The girls gave a little scream and then ran away from her. The fly, seated on a dish of preserves, was eating comfortably, greedily sucking up the luscious syrup. She saw the butterfly fall, but was in no way disturbed; there was a large quantity of preserves, and she enjoyed them greatly. When our poor little thing came to herself she was still lying on the nosegay, and her friend the spider was standing over her, shaking his burly form sorrowfully; he had already made a small web over her head.

"How did you get here, my friend?" asked she in a dying voice.

"I was dragged here against my will. When they cut the twigs of honeysuckle I was on them, as ill luck would have it, and was brought here with them. But it's very lucky for you, my poor little one, all the same."

But the butterfly, having shut her eyes, did not hear her friend's last words. It was night, and the lights had gone out. The butterfly was lying with her poor burnt wings, suffering dreadful agony and incapable of moving. The spider had left her, too, without a word. She was dying alone, abandoned by everyone. But soon she heard the heavy step of her friend, accompanied by a plaintive buzzing from the blue-bottle. Turning her eyes in that direction, she saw in the moonlight that the spider had come to a settlement with his blue enemy: having rolled her up in a web from head to foot, he set to work comfortably, and without saying one word, to make her into three dishes, soup, roast, and dessert, and having supped in this manner he seated himself close to the suffering butterfly.

I have heard that after long suffering she regained her health, though she had lost all her beauty, and that she refrained from making further acquaintanceship with flies; but the spider, they say, never abandoned her.

PRINCESS SILLYKIN.

"GENTLY, gently," said the ladies-in-waiting as they entered the luxurious hall of a magnificent palace.

"What is it?" inquired a court dignitary.

"The empress is unwell," whispered they almost inaudibly. "It appears that to-day she will give us an heir."

"Ah! if it could only be a princess!" said a young and pretty lady. "I like little girls so much!"

At this moment the door was opened and the empress's old nurse led all the ladies into the sleeping chamber. A daughter was born to the empress. The young lady who liked little girls was delighted, but the courtiers were dissatisfied. The emperor himself seemed a little put out; he had wanted an heir. But, on the other hand, how happy was the empress!

She lay on a richly-covered bed; the curtains were of fine lace, the bedstead of glistening mother-of-pearl covered with snow-white counter-panes of silver lace.

Behind a screen the old nurse was attending to the little princess. She was wrapping and covering her up to bring her to the empress.

"Let my daughter be brought to me at once," said the beautiful empress; "I want to kiss her directly."

At that moment the nurse came from behind the screen holding with both hands a tiny crystal saucer; the new-born baby lay in the saucer, covered with one rose leaf.

"What!" shrieked the empress; "can this be my daughter, such a tiny little thing?"

"But look what a beauty she is!" said the nurse; "could there be a greater darling than this?"

They gave the little princess to her mother, who held her in the palm of one hand and indulged in admiration of her little one. All the ladies of the court were allowed to look at her, and each of them, approaching the princess, kissed the edge of the rose leaf.

Feeling that her swaddling-clothes were disturbed the princess began crying, but with such a melodious voice that it sounded like the tinkling of small silver bells.

"How strange it is!" said the courtiers. "No

one ever saw such a tiny thing in the whole kingdom."

But the empress was so pleased with her little daughter that she would not allow her to be absent from her for one minute.

The old nurse brought a small cradle made of a pink shell, and filling it with swan-down she covered it with a white lily petal, and put the princess to bed, placing the cradle on a little table near the empress.

What a strange child it was! Whilst still but a baby she gave signs of a capricious disposition. She never took her natural food without screaming so long afterwards that they did not know what to do with her. But as she showed pleasure in sucking the rose leaf with which she was covered her mother guessed that she wished to suck the juice of flowers and had her cradle placed in the centre of a nosegay.

Every day the empress bathed her little daughter in a white shell with pearly rims. The princess appeared to prefer water to everything, and crowed with joy when bathed.

"Now, my child," said the old nurse to the empress one day, "we shall have trouble with this whimsical little thing. I never in my life saw such a fanciful child."

"Oh, nurse! how can you say such a thing?'

exclaimed the empress. "She is so tiny still, and therefore but a silly little thing Don't cry, then, don't cry," said she to her daughter; "you're my own little sillykin."

And indeed everyone called the princess "Little Sillykin," and so they christened her, with the permission of the empress.

But the princess grew and grew, but without becoming at all wiser. She wouldn't hear of learning lessons. The empress tried hard to teach her to read, but in vain; the princess only indulged in fresh whims. She turned the handsome binding of her primer into a house, or else, leaning the book against the wall, she let herself slide down it as if it had been a hill-slope.

Although she went on growing she still remained very tiny.

Her poor mother shed many tears over her little whimsical daughter. There was nothing she did not try. Imagining that Little Sillykin was ill she assembled all the doctors of the kingdom. They looked at the child on every side, undressed her, sounded her chest, examined her, and shook their heads. The case appeared to them far from simple, and they were already preparing to write out prescriptions, when suddenly Sillykin escaped from their hands, began hopping about the table, sang a song in her ringing voice, and then put out her tongue to the learned assembly.

"She is simply full of wilfulness," declared the doctors, and retired in dudgeon.

One day the poor empress had taken her little daughter in her hands and began to talk to her and admonish her on her being so different from other children.

"Look here, Sillykin," said the empress, "even our housemaid's children are wiser than you, although their father and mother are very poor and can't do anything for their education. Every day I see with pleasure from the window how tiny little girls, younger than yourself, help their mothers in their household work, and never give way to temper."

"There are a great many of them, mama, and I am alone. I feel sad. I should like to have the prettiest little boy in the kingdom to be with me, and then I should not feel so lonely; but I want him to be the very curliest, pinkest, and prettiest, and I won't have him ugly, I won't, I won't, I won't!"

Here the princess stamped with her tiny little foot and began to shed tears.

"Don't, oh, don't!" said her mother tenderly, "I have not offered you an ugly one. You shall have your pretty little boy."

The empress then left her.

Messengers were sent all over the kingdom to find the desired little boy. The empress gave severe orders that they should find not only the prettiest, but the best little boy. She knew that it would be very hard for him to live with Sillykin unless he were full of goodness and gentleness.

They searched throughout the kingdom, but after a week's time they found what they wanted.

He was really a beautiful little boy. His glossy light hair curled all over his head and formed a thick lock just above his forehead. His little face and forehead were as white as snow and his cheeks as red as poppies, whilst his dark eyes shone out from beneath long black eyelashes. His little mouth reminded you of a ripe cherry, and his whole face glowed with such kindness that whoever looked at him at once loved the beautiful child. He was always dressed in a short white blouse, with white trousers, and a broad gold belt.

He was beautiful, there was no doubt about it.

As soon as Sillykin saw him she sprang into his arms.

"Dear, wonderful, little Curlyhead," exclaimed she, "I will always, always love you, and will never leave you."

"Very well," answered the little Curlyhead, "and I'll love you." Upon which they embraced one another warmly and exchanged kisses.

In the garden the princess had had a little house built in which she always played, such a charming, pretty, little house. It was made of pink crystal, the roof was of silver, the floor was strewn with golden sand, and its tiny furniture was of mother-of-pearl. There was a small set of household utensils in the house, and in one of the rooms had been built a large cage, surrounded with silver lace of extremely fine tissue, and in this cage lived a quantity of the tiniest birds of variegated colours, whose feathers reflected the most brilliant tints. Every day Sillykin went to feed them. She took two buckets, which were made of large hollow pearls. In one of them she put the seed, and she filled the other with sweetened water, and raising the silver lace of the cage she went inside amidst the birds.

They all knew her, and came to drink and eat from her hand. But usually even this tired Sillykin, and suddenly, for this or that reason, she would dash the bucket on the floor, spilling the water, and wasting the seed, and wetting herself; and then, thoroughly angry, she would run home in her wet clothes, crying bitterly.

To this house the princess brought her companion. The little boy was delighted with everything, but when he saw the birds he fell into a perfect ecstasy. He took the buckets and set to work feeding them.

Sillykin for the first time gave up this pleasure to the little boy. With delight in his brilliant eyes Curlyhead seized a bucket, seated himself on the floor, and scattered the seed; the birds flew to him and began to peck. He sat quite still, afraid to move, and when they had eaten up everything he gave them the bucket of water and remained quiet again.

When they had drunk sufficiently the birds began to sing, and two small humming-birds seated themselves on the little boy's shoulder. Soon they began to circle round him, and in emulation of one another tried to perch on or near him. At last he was completely covered with them, and sat motionless not to alarm them. His face was glowing with pleasure, his eyes sparkled, and his half-opened mouth wore a sweet smile.

The princess stood gazing at him; but soon she felt mortified, because the birds never played with her like that. She stamped her little foot and screamed:

"Nasty birds!" With these words she dashed out of the cage, tearing the silver lace with her foot in the extremity of her rage.

Curlyhead sprang up in alarm and ran after her. He just overtook Sillykin on the large marble stairs which led to the sea.

In spite of all he could say to her she kept on crying and screaming:

"Nasty birds! Nasty house! I'll never go to it again. The first time you went there they loved you. Go every day and feed them. They always fly away from me to the furthermost corner. They only come near when I have food in my hands."

"You evidently frighten them; they are afraid of you. Do you love them sufficiently, Sillykin?"

"No. I can't bear them," said the princess spitefully.

Curlyhead turned his eyes on her in astonishment.

"You must certainly be unwell. Yes, you are really unwell, my poor little one."

He kissed her, took her carefully in his hands, and carried her up the staircase. Then he placed Sillykin in the garden under a large orange-tree, on the grass, and seated himself beside her. For a long time he kissed her and soothed her, still persuaded that she was suffering; but the princess sulked and would not return his caresses.

Suddenly she slipped from him and ran away. The boy pursued her, and caught her near a large flower-bed, where grew the most beautiful flowers.

There were so many of them that little Curly-head jumped about and clapped his hands with joy.

"Sillykin," he screamed, "I'll at once make you a wreath of lilies of the valley, a frock of a red poppy, and shoes of violets. Sit down here for a minute."

Sillykin sat down, and her face became brighter.

"I feel very hot," she said.

"Be patient," said Curlyhead. "I'll arrange something for you. Would you like to bathe?"

"Yes, I should."

"Well, then, undress."

In the flower-bed grew a beautiful white rose-bush. One of its blossoms was very large and quite besprinkled with fresh dew. Its cup contained such a quantity that Curlyhead carefully took the undressed Sillykin in his hands, and seated her in its depths.

The cool dew at once refreshed her. She began to laugh and rejoice, and tumble about in the water, whilst Curlyhead was preparing her fresh attire.

"The dew has grown hot," she cried; "splash me with fresh."

The little boy plucked a lily, and, bending it over Sillykin's head, a thread of fresh perfumed water fell over her.

"Now it's time to come out," said Curlyhead; "here, let me dress you." Then he adorned her with her poppy gown and her violet shoes.

"Now, sit upon a leaf," said he, "and be careful not to climb down alone."

"No! I will climb down, I'll climb down by myself," screamed Sillykin as she slipped down. No sooner had Curlyhead succeeded in catching her than she twisted herself round a twig, scratched her little leg, and began screaming violently.

Curlyhead was frightened, and knew not what to do. He held her in his hands, and ran across the garden straight to the empress. The empress was frightened also; she put the princess in her mother-of-pearl cradle, and wrapped up her scratched leg in a rose-leaf. The cradle was hung by silver cords in a little bush, and Curlyhead rocked it until the suffering Sillykin fell asleep.

On awaking, her pain was gone. She put on her violet boots and jumped down.

"It is hot," she screamed in an angry voice. "I don't want it to be summer. The flowers all scratch. The sun roasts. I want winter. I want to slide down the hills. I want it to be cold."

"But how can one have winter in summer?" asked Curlyhead. "Please don't scream, Sillykin.

There's no use in asking for what can't be had. You only torment mama."

"I will have winter," screamed Sillykin angrily. "Mama, make it winter;" and she stamped her foot.

The nearly-closed wound reopened, and a drop of red blood fell from her leg. The empress clasped her hands in dismay.

"Oh, oh! she will be quite ill," cried she with tears; "what shall I do?"

"Winter, I want winter!" went on screaming Sillykin, becoming rapidly feverish.

"Very well, very well," said her mother soothingly; "only be quiet, little silly thing, and I'll arrange it somehow."

"No; say that it will be winter to-morrow," said the princess wilfully. "I shall die if it is not winter to-morrow."

"It shall be winter to-morrow," said the bewildered empress, and Sillykin fell asleep. Curlyhead also lay down to sleep in the nursery.

The children slept soundly all night, and awoke late. After breakfasting on fresh fruit they ran to the empress. She was delighted to see that her child was quite well.

"Now, then, Sillykin, do you still wish for winter?"

"I want it, mama," answered the little girl.

"I've already told you that I positively will have it."

"And will you be a good girl to-day if I make winter for you?" pursued the empress.

"Certainly I will," said the flighty Sillykin.

"Well, I'm very glad of it. Go to the garden, and there you'll see pretty things."

The children ran off to the spot where the fountain was. Sillykin ran with all her might, but she was so small that she could not keep up with Curlyhead. She was beginning to get angry with him for this, but she remembered that she had just promised her mother to be good.

At the turn of the road the children stopped, with eyes wide opened, and mute with astonishment. Before them stood a large house built entirely of transparent rock-crystal. The roof was covered with silver stars, and all the walls were hung with a web of silver threads. They opened the door and entered.

The floor of the large hall was covered with a carpet of swan-down and feathers. The transparent walls were hung with a silver netting. The large blue crystal windows were covered with slender diamond sprays, and beneath them hung large pearls in clusters. All these things were entwined and interwoven in the most marvellous manner.

H

In the middle of the hall a large sky-blue lake had been contrived of polished crystal, and into a corner of it flowed a spring of clear water. This lake was indeed cold. On its crystal surface stood two pairs of golden skates, and on one side a smooth slope was arranged, made of silver stars covered with white glass. At the top of the slope were two sledges, the one of ivory for Curlyhead, and the other made out of a shell for Sillykin.

Under the brilliant surface of the blue lake swam and gambolled golden fishes.

The light of the hall was blue. There was no ceiling whatever, and through the silver stars of the roof the blue sky was visible, and the fresh morning wind gliding between them set in movement the clusters of pearls of the windows and the silver netting of the wall. The crystal drapery of the artificial slope rang gently, and the pearls clinked in harmony as they moved in the breeze.

How charming and quiet was that blue hall! The splashing of the fishes against the surface of the lake alone was heard, with the murmur of the water against its blue channel.

Sillykin sprang gaily on the lake, fastened on the golden skates, and started off. Curlyhead climbed up the slope, seated himself in a sledge, and slided down to meet her. Sillykin laughed and enjoyed herself, gliding over the smooth crystal on her skates, whilst Curlyhead rushed down the steep slope.

After having enjoyed herself enough, Sillykin ran to him and said:

"Winter is better than everything; it shall be mine. You can take summer. I make you a present of my pink house with the birds."

Curlyhead was excessively pleased; he kissed Sillykin and said:

"If so I must also give you something."

He unbuttoned his little blouse, took from his neck a golden string from which hung three large pearls, and gave it to Sillykin.

"Take these pearls," said he; "my mother gave them to me, and told me to open the first of them when I wished to know all that is necessary for life; from the second can be learnt whatever is necessary for happiness; and from the third, whatever is useful. But she told me only to open each of them as it was needed."

"Very well," said Sillykin, fastening the string round her throat. She kissed Curlyhead and at once forgot all about her gift, for she had not yet been on the sledges, and of course she must try them.

Curlyhead did not regret his pearls; he loved Sillykin more than himself, and wished her to have everything that was best.

Having had enough of sledging, Sillykin suddenly became sulky and ran away. She wished to hide from everything; but her conscience reminded her that she had promised her mother to be good, and she had broken her word.

But Curlyhead found her and tried to talk her over. To all his words she only answered:

"It's a bore; the winter and everything else is tiresome. You are tiresome too."

Curlyhead turned aside sadly and left the place, and Sillykin ran away to the marble staircase and went down to the sea.

She began to look at the water, and saw a small fish who was caught between the stones and could not escape into the open sea. Sillykin looked at the little fish and suddenly began to pity him. This surprised her, for until then she had never thought of anything but herself.

She bent down and plunged her little hand up to the elbow into the cold water, but she could not catch the fish. She then resolved to enter the water with her little feet, and though she wet her frock still she caught the fish, and threw him into the blue sea.

Feeling himself at liberty, the fish beat the water joyously with his tail and vanished beneath the surface.

"How pleasant it must be in the sea!" said

Sillykin. "The best thing I can do is to escape to the fishes; it must be very jolly there, and I am tired of everything here. I should like to see what life is like in the sea."

With these words the princess brought to the shore a large clear shell, one half of which could be closed over the other, placed it in the water near the steps, seated herself in it, and, pushing off with a little stick, floated away on the wide sea.

Long did Curlyhead search for his Sillykin and long did the empress weep for her, but no one could find the princess. Meanwhile she floated on the deep blue sea, looking in all directions for the kingdom of the fishes.

The shell began to rock violently. Now lifted up on a huge wave it mounted high above the surface, and now sinking low it was surrounded by the water as if it had been in the centre of a funnel. Sillykin was much frightened, and hardly had she managed to fasten down the lid of her shell when she felt it sinking rapidly, rapidly towards the bottom of the sea.

The poor princess closed her eyes from fright, nor did she open them until her little boat reached the sandy bottom.

The shell drove its dentilated edges deep into the sand and stopped short.

The princess opened her frightened eyes, and,

gazing through the transparent walls of her dwelling, saw many wonderful things. On every side she was surrounded by the dark-green water; high, high over her head it rose, and the shattered light of the sun's golden rays illumined its depths. A thick forest of coral, the end of which was invisible, rose above her. Through the pointed interwoven branches the water rippled in crystal streams. The glittering sand was strewn with the strangest shells, shedding from their half-open cups large white pearls, and moving amidst the gold-like amber, of which large lumps grew up from the bottom of the sea. Strange flowers and plants were entwined with the shells, all of the most vivid colours, and throwing out on all sides slender and pliant shoots; they waved gently in the water, now opening and now closing. The fishes moved in shoals, and the sea-snails crawled in myriads; it was evident that the bottom of the sea was full of inhabitants.

Sillykin gazed in every direction astonished, and thinking that it was pleasant amongst the fishes. On every side her eyes saw something new and she felt glad that she had fallen to the bottom of the sea. But suddenly it began to grow dark, the golden rays of the sun were effaced from the water and extinguished with the rapidity of lightning.

It began to be dark at the bottom of the sea. The princess saw nothing more, she only heard above her head the dull whisper and murmur of the great sea. Everything slumbered in its depths; Sillykin alone was sleepless. She felt alarmed, and although she tried hard to sleep, sleep came not to her. So she passed the whole night, tired out with watching and longing for food. But what was to be done? where was food to be had?

"Ah! if they would only give me a small piece of bread," thought Sillykin with tears. "I never wanted to eat it when at home, but fed upon sugar-plums and fruit; but now I would eat bread like the housemaid's children. But, alas! I have none. I see quantities of pearls and precious things, but what are they to me? I am dying of hunger and thirst. If I could sleep at least; but that too is out of the question. No! I see now that precious things are not what is necessary for life."

Bitterly sobbed Sillykin, but suddenly she thought of her pearls, and remembered what Curlyhead had told her about opening one of them when she wanted to know what was necessary for life. She at once seized a pearl, opened it, and saw that it contained three things, a grain of corn, a drop of water, and a poppy seed. With trembling hands she seized and ate the grain of corn, and her hunger left her; she then drank the drop of water, and her thirst was quenched.

She felt infinitely lighter and gayer. But what was to be done with the poppy seed? Sillykin after a little reflection resolved to eat it. Hardly had she swallowed it than she fell into a deep sleep.

Sillykin saw nothing more, nor was she aware how long she slept; but when she awoke the sun played so gaily on the water that far, far away, everything was visible on the bottom of the sea. The pellucid water rose and fell with the golden rays that illumined its depths.

Sillykin sat thinking in her shell: "It is pleasant at the bottom of the sea, and I love to look at its wonders. But how am I to live here? I can't leave the shell."

"If I were at home mama would care for me. Who is there to love me here? I know no one down here, nor is there any one to know. I can't be happy alone with no one to love me. How silly I am, how silly! Why did I ever come to the bottom of the sea? I never even thought of the possibility of my being unable to live here. Now, I have learnt what is needful for life: bread, not to die of hunger; fresh water, not to perish from thirst; and sleep, for repose. What then is necessary for happiness?"

She again began to cry, and then she thought of the other pearl. She quickly opened it, and found inside it a small golden cross with the inscription, "Love others like thyself."

Poor Sillykin with great trouble made out the inscription, syllable by syllable. She managed it at last, after recalling, by an effort, the whole alphabet.

Sillykin reflected more and more.

"It appears that one must love others like one's self," considered she; "that is what is needful for happiness." She recalled her whole life with her mother, and was terrified; she had loved no one save only herself. That was why life was so tiresome to her, and she had not felt happy. She felt so sorry for her mother and father, and even her old nurse. It was the first time she had felt any pity for them. She burst into tears no longer for herself but for them.

But suddenly she remembered that once in her life she had pitied a little golden fish and replaced it in the deep water; her heart beat with joy at this remembrance.

"Yes, it is indeed happiness to love others," she said aloud; "come you at least, little golden fish, and I will love you."

Her shell was strongly shaken. Sillykin looked out, and saw a small fish digging up the sand with its head and setting the shell free. When its edge was loosened from the deep sand the fish hooked his tail to one of the ridges and began to rise rapidly with the shell.

With extraordinary rapidity passed before Sillykin the pearl shells, the shoals of fishes, the floating plants, and the coral forests. She rose to the surface, lighted up by the sunbeams. But the little golden fish still glistened before her, the very same she had saved and loved.

Hardly had Sillykin time to draw a breath than the shell struck strongly against something and stopped. The fish opened the lid of the shell with his tail, and Sillykin found herself near the marble steps of her garden.

On the top of the staircase sat the poor empress embracing Curlyhead. The latter was drying her tears with his dimpled hands and consoling her.

Sillykin sprang upon the steps, rushed upstairs, and threw herself into the arms of the empress and Curlyhead. They all three wept and laughed for joy. Curlyhead felt so happy that you could see sparks dancing in his eyes.

They all went to the emperor, who was also filled with delight, and ordered the band to play the whole day in the garden, and the bells to be rung, that the whole empire might know and rejoice with them that the Princess Sillykin was found.

The emperor seated Sillykin on his knee and requested her to tell him all that had happened to her. She related everything that had occurred, and added that she would never forget the pearls, but would always bear in mind what was necessary for life and happiness.

"Now I shall eat bread and everything like other people," said she. "Then I sha'n't be ill, and shall grow up rapidly. I shall also love every one, every one; yes, I already love every one," added she, kissing her father, and mother, and Curlyhead; and then she ran off to her old nurse.

"Forgive me, dear nurse," said she; "I have done nothing but worry and torment you; but now it won't be for you to look after me, but I shall take care of you. Lie quietly on your bed, dear nurse, I'll no longer trouble and disturb you at night. I know that sleep is needful for life, my pearl has taught it me;" and throwing her arms round her nurse's neck she kissed her wrinkled old cheeks.

"So that's how it is, my beautiful sunbeam," said the nurse with joy; "so at last you have taken to be good. You are no longer a baby; it is time for you to learn and time to think of work. That is what will be useful for you now."

"And what is needed to be useful?" thought Sillykin. In all haste she opened the third shell, which contained what was useful, a flax seed and a small alphabet.

"It is then necessary to work and study," said she presently. "Yes, dear nurse, you are right; I will spin thread of flax, I will sew and help mama and you, like the housemaid's daughter, and I will learn to study and to be good like little Curlyhead."

And with these words she fastened her little cross to the golden chain instead of the pearls.

And truly Princess Sillykin kept her word. She loved every one, and studied and worked regardless of fatigue; she could soon read pretty stories fluently and agreeably to her friend Curlyhead. Every one loved her, every one praised her goodness of heart. She was never capricious now, nor did she cause her mama to shed tears. Her old nurse slept quietly all night long, and began to grow young again.

She ate everything, and began to grow rapidly, so that soon she was only a little smaller than Curlyhead. The little boy loved her so much that he could never leave her.

After some years had passed thus, the emperor made known to the whole country that there would soon be a wedding; the Princess Sillykin was to marry young Curlyhead.

The whole kingdom was delighted, for the young couple loved every one almost as much as they loved one another.

Sillykin sewed a pretty wedding outfit for herself. One day before the wedding Curlyhead took his betrothed to the birds in the crystal house. There he seated her on a mother-of-pearl arm-chair and said: "My dearest princess, accept my wedding gift."

He gave her a green acorn. On opening it she found a dozen pocket handkerchiefs of the finest cambric. Each of them bore in the finest embroidery the princess's coronet, and round it was written "*Princess Darling*."

"You are no longer to be called Sillykin," said Curlyhead; "I give you a new name—'Darling.'"

"We give you the name of 'Darling,'" sang the birds.

The wind took up the words and carried them to the garden.

"Princess Darling," repeated the beetles and the butterflies. "Princess Darling," rang the crystal drapery of the winter house. "Darling," tinkled the clusters of pearls. The flowers greeted her, and whispered the same words.

The wind bore it all over the kingdom, and to the blue sea, until the new name was proclaimed everywhere.

The sea was agitated, and from wave to wave rolled the fame of "*Princess Darling.*"

THE END.

CPSIA information can be obtained
at www.ICGtesting.com
Printed in the USA
BVHW070408020119
536776BV00012B/1220/P